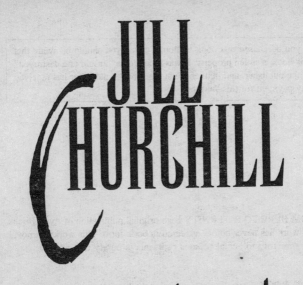

JILL CHURCHILL

From Here to Paternity

A JANE JEFFRY MYSTERY

AVON BOOKS ◆ NEW YORK

FROM HERE TO PATERNITY is an original publication of Avon Books. This work has never before appeared in book form. This work is a novel. Any similarity to actual persons or events is purely coincidental.

AVON BOOKS
A division of
The Hearst Corporation
1350 Avenue of the Americas
New York, New York 10019

First Avon Books Printing: July 1995

AVON TRADEMARK REG. U.S. PAT. OFF. AND IN OTHER COUNTRIES, MARCA REGISTRADA, HECHO EN U.S.A.

Printed in the U.S.A.

RA 10 9 8 7 6 5 4 3 2 1

This book is dedicated to all the other genealogists who have been such a help to me—especially Caroll Geerling, who so generously gave me all those Webers.

"Jill Churchill"
a.k.a. Janice Brooks
Searching for:
  YOUNG (Switzerland to PA, KS)
  WALKER, WILLIAMS (Delaware tribe, MD, IN, KS)
  LITHGOW, McCONNELL (Britain to PA)
  MORING, THOMPSON (Nova Scotia to WV)
  APPEL (Hesse Kassel to NJ, PA)
  SCHMID (Germany to NJ, PA)
  PFEIFFER, WELLER (Germany to MO)
  DOVE, HILSKOR (Prussia to MO)
  VINING (England to MO)
  JONES (Bainbridge, County Down to PA)
  McCOY, WILHOITE, TODD (East TN)
  WEBER (Alsace to MO)
  FREILER, WERTZ (Bavaria to PA)
  WEIRATHER, FISHER (Germany to MO)

internet email addresses:
COZYBOOKS@DELPHI.COM
JYBROOKS@TYRELL.NET

"All we need now is a roaring fire and a bottle of wine," Jane Jeffry said contentedly as she looked out the window at the snow.

"I've never found a rental car with a fireplace," Mel VanDyne said, hunching over the steering wheel and glaring into darkness.

"I didn't mean 'now' now. I mean when we get there."

"Which will probably be well into the next century at the rate we're going. Do you realize that we left Chicago at six o'clock and it's now almost eleven and we're still not there? We could have flown to London instead of Colorado in this time. And we probably wouldn't be stuck in a blinding blizzard, either."

"Now, Mel. It's not exactly blinding. You can see all sorts of— Oh, my God! What's *that* thing?"

Mel slowed the car to a crawl. "I think it's an elk."

A herd of extremely large, hoofed animals were near the side of the highway and one had wandered out into the slow lane, apparently to amuse and alarm tourists. Fortunately, there was practically no other traffic on the interstate and Mel could slow down without being rear-ended. The big animal shambled off before Mel had to come to a complete stop.

"Wow! What a great-looking animal!" Jane exclaimed. "It's a good thing we were going so slowly. Imagine if you hit something like that."

Mel nodded. "Yeah. It'd be like clipping the Sears Tower. Only bloodier."

"Look, Willard! Wild animals," Jane chirped over her shoulder.

There was a muffled dog groan from the backseat.

"Are you sure that dog's all right?" Mel said.

"It's just the tranquilizer the vet had me give him before we left. I knew he'd be scared by the plane ride, so I really doped him up."

"If he were any dopier, he'd have to be reclassified as a vegetable. Why did you have to bring him?"

"Well, it was that or put him in the kennel, and he's never been to a kennel. He'd think we'd abandoned him, poor old guy. Watch it or I'll give you one of his pills." She slipped into a bad Peter Lorre imitation: "I have drugs and I know how to use them."

"I've worked hard at nursing along this bad mood. Don't you dare try to take it away from me," Mel snarled.

Jane waved this warning off. "Until you've had a teenage daughter, you don't know what a bad mood really is. You haven't even got to the learner permit stage of tantrums. I think there's a town just ahead. There might be something open where you could get a cup of coffee," she added.

They took the off-ramp and found a single, glaringly lighted convenience store open. Mel went in to buy coffee while Jane studied the map of Colorado. Yes, another twenty miles, maybe thirty, she thought, then cringed as she looked up and saw Mel talking with the convenience-store clerk. Lots of pointing. Hmmm. He was asking directions. Not a good sign. Men never seemed to resort to asking for help except when really stressed. And then they didn't listen anyway.

This was a side of him she hadn't seen in the year and a half they'd been dating. Well, dating in a manner of speaking. They'd first met when Jane's next-door neighbor and best friend, Shelley, found a dead cleaning lady in her guest bedroom and Mel was the detective assigned to the case. More often than not during that first year, Jane and Mel had met as witness and police officer. Or police officer and neighborhood busybody, as Mel would probably interpret it. He was always the cool, calm bachelor and Jane was the frazzled, widowed mother of three, trying to keep her whole life from flying off in random bits of car pools, PTA business, teenage fits of angst, and algebra homework. Being the one *not* going to pieces was rather refreshing!

When he got back with a pair of steaming Styrofoam cups, he said, "I can't help but notice that you're taking this nightmare journey awfully well."

Jane smiled. "Well, I grew up a State Department brat. When you've lived practically everywhere in the world, you get used to travel catastrophes. And this one doesn't even qualify. Nothing's really even gone wrong. It's just taken a lot of time. That's nothing. I once had a camel eat my favorite doll. Even rental-car clerks seldom get that surly."

Mel took a sip of his overcooked convenience-store coffee and grimaced. "I keep forgetting that about you. Well, not forgetting, exactly—"

"You might want to explain that," Jane said. "I think you just wandered onto dangerous turf."

Mel grinned. "It's not an insult. At least I didn't mean it as one. I just meant that you're usually so—so domestic. So grounded in your family and house and pets and neighborhood. And then there's this other Jane—the one I've seen today—who can pack up an idiot dog, and a couple small suitcases and calmly take off. You didn't get rattled or nasty over the airplane seat mix-up, you just sorted it out. You seem to be able to read maps in the dark. You don't appear to be bothered by the fact that we're high in the mountains, in a blizzard, and likely to starve to death—"

Jane laughed. "Us and the Donner party. Mel, we're parked in front of a convenience store. And my map-reading skills, which you admire so much, tell me that we've got another half hour at least and had better get going."

"Tell me again why in hell we're doing this," Mel said as he backtracked to the highway ramp.

"Because of Shelley Nowack's husband, Paul. He invests in things. And some group wants him to put a bunch of money into investing in this resort. Somebody or other—I'm not clear on whether it was the other investors or the current owners of the place—wanted to knock his socks off with what a great place it is and offered him and eight of his nearest and dearest a free extended weekend. Including airfare, which was really generous. You and I qualify as two of Paul's nearest and dearest."

Mel grinned. "That would probably surprise Paul Nowack to learn, being as he doesn't even know me."

"But he knows of you. And for the sake of this trip, you count as part of my family."

"I'm just a humble cop—"

"Hardly humble," Jane muttered.

"—not a high-stakes real estate entrepreneur, but it seems to me that this place is likely to be a real hell-hole if somebody's willing to go to all that trouble and expense to unload it."

"Oh, no. I saw the brochures. It's a fantastic place. But there is something—"

Mel's eyes widened in alarm. "Oh?"

"Well, it seems it's a ski resort without a mountain. That's what Shelley said."

"Without a mountain? Jane, even in the dark I can tell we're surrounded by mountains. They're great hulking things with pointy tops and thousands of tons of snow poised to avalanche down on us. You can hardly miss them."

"This resort's *in* the mountains, it just doesn't have one of its very own. But it has everything else you'd want for a vacation, they say. That was the point in inviting both our families. To show off all the fun stuff you can do at this resort."

"Except ski."

"Right. And you can ski, Shelley says. Just not right there. You take a shuttle bus that runs every fifteen minutes to a place just two miles down the road that's supposed to have terrific skiing."

Mel was unconvinced. "And we're not even staying together. You and I, I mean."

"I told you, Shelley has to entertain these investors in the condo she's been given and couldn't have all the kids underfoot. And there's no way either of us would trust the kids to stay alone."

Mel shook his head. "So let me see if I've got this straight. We're going to a ski resort without a mountain to have a romantic weekend—except that you're bunking with your daughter and Shelley's and I'm in with the male offspring of both families. And on top of all that, we're lost in the middle of the night in a blizzard with an unconscious dog in the backseat."

Jane considered, nodding pleasantly. "That's about it. Yes. I think you've hit the main points rather succinctly. Except that we're not really lost and you left out that it's free."

"Of course it's free! You don't think anybody'd pay money for this situation do you?"

Jane unlatched her seat belt, scooted across the seat, and kissed his cheek. "Mel, maybe you ought to switch to decaf."

Jane's next-door neighbor and best friend, Shelley, had arrived with her husband and all the children of both families earlier the same day. Shelley was waiting at the front desk when Jane and Mel finally arrived at a few minutes after midnight. "I was getting worried about you!"

"You were just worried that you'd get stuck with all the kids," Jane said.

"There was that," Shelley admitted. "Come on, I'll show you both where you're staying."

They drove from the main lodge up a narrow, winding road edged with pines that were bowed down with snow. At a wooden sign saying, "Eagle's Nest," which, due to fancy lettering, Jane took to be saying, "Bagle's Nest," Shelley told Mel to turn into a parking lot. Four luxurious homes surrounded the small lot. "Paul and I are in the first one, you and the girls are in the second one, Jane, and Mel and the boys are in the one at the far end."

"These are the cabins?" Jane exclaimed. "They're nicer than my house!"

"Each one is a duplex, though you wouldn't guess it to look. Your entrance is on this side," Shelley said, pointing.

"Help me with Willard, and then you'll be finished with me for the day," Jane told Mel.

"Finished with you and starting with the boys," he groused.

"Don't worry about them," Shelley said. "They skied all afternoon and are probably sound asleep. Jane's got the tough lot. Girls can go for phenomenal lengths of time without sleeping."

It took all three of them to unload Willard and wake him up enough that he wobbled over to a tree to lift his leg. Jane had to lean against the big shambling yellow dog to keep him from falling right over while he teetered on three legs. As soon as they had him headed toward the right door, Shelley gave Mel his key. He gave Jane a perfunctory kiss and started unloading his own luggage.

"Mr. Conviviality," Shelley muttered, unlocking Jane's door while Jane fought to get Willard back on his feet. He'd decided to sleep on the step.

"He's a tad cranky from the drive. It *is* a terribly long way from the Denver airport, and the drive up into the mountains is horrifying at night in the snow. Besides, I think he's afraid of flying and much too macho to admit it. I thought there was something wrong with the engines until I realized it was just Mel grinding his teeth."

"Voilà!" Shelley said, flinging the door open.

Jane dragged Willard inside and let him collapse in the front hall before she took a look around.

"My God! What a place!" she exclaimed.

There was a large living room with a sunken seating area in front of a fireplace that would have been at home in a largish castle. A pile of logs glowed red and filled the room with the delicious scent of woodsmoke. The fireplace wall was of slabs of fieldstone. The far end of the room was entirely glass, with doors that opened onto a deck that wrapped around the back of the structure. The wall between was entirely shelves, with books, handsome knickknacks, and an entertainment center that included a huge television, VCR, and tape deck. The rich forest-green carpeting, dark wood, and deeply upholstered leather furniture combined to be both sumptuous and rustic. Jane was grinning until she turned around to look at Shelley and spotted what was behind them.

"Oh, no! What's that!"

"You know what it is."

"I hope I'm wrong, but it looks suspiciously like a *kitchen!* Curses!"

"Now, Jane. You don't ever have to go in it if you don't want to."

"Shelley, don't be an idiot. Where there's a kitchen and a mother, people will expect cooking to be done."

"Then those unnamed people will just have to live with disappointment for a few days," Shelley said.

"I know. That firewood on the deck. Maybe we could use that to board it up and nobody will ever know it's there."

"Too late. I already took the girls to the grocery store and they've filled it with soft drinks and junk food. And I've stashed a lovely bottle of white wine and some of your favorite cheese in the fridge. Want a glass?"

"If you'll fix it," Jane said. "I want to leave here without ever having set foot in that room."

She hauled her bag and Willard down the hall, observing with approval that her daughter, Katie, and Shelley's daughter, Denise, shared a big bedroom, while she had a smaller but more attractive one with its own bath all to herself. Her bedroom had two queen-sized beds with room left over. It also had a glass wall overlooking the deck. She greeted the girls, who were shrieking with laughter and trying out a dreadful mauve shade of nail polish, before taking off her travel clothes and donning a comfortable flannel granny gown and fuzzy slippers. As a child, she'd always been "representing her country" when she traveled and couldn't break the habit of dressing up to get on a plane. Someday she might be able to throw on a pair of jeans and head for the airport, but for now, she was stuck with dresses and hose. She hung up her dress and a few other items that were in her suitcase, then found an extra blanket in the closet and made a nest at the foot of the bed for Willard.

By the time she returned to the living room, Shelley was stirring up the embers of the fire and had set out two glasses of wine and a little plate of Wheat Thins and a section of Brie. "You sure know the way to a girl's heart," Jane said, collapsing into the big, deep armchair closest to the fire.

Shelley looked at her. "You can disintegrate faster than anyone I've ever known."

"I know," Jane said smugly. "It's a gift. So how's it going? Is Paul going to buy this place?"

"I have no idea. He and the other investors spent the day just looking around. Tomorrow they're going over all the paperwork and financial statements. The owner's niece, a really nice woman around our age named Tenny Garner, has put herself in charge of us. If there's anything you need, just call the front desk and ask for her."

"Shelley, the place looked deserted as we drove in."

"No, it's really not. For one thing, it's awfully late, and for another, the whole place is arranged in such a way that everything seems very isolated and private and disguises the fact that you're surrounded by mobs of people. That's one of the advantages."

"But, Shelley, who comes to a ski resort without ski facilities—besides you and me and other people dedicated to the sedentary life?"

"Conventions. Right now there's a gang of accountants just getting ready to leave, the regional representatives of an agricultural co-op arriving in a couple days, and some kind of historical society meeting now. They're a tad bizarre. If you run into a woman who looks like Abe Lincoln in drag, you might want to veer off before she can bend your ear."

"I think if I spotted such a person I'd hide on general principles without the warning. But thanks anyway," Jane said, yawning. "So what's the plan for tomorrow?"

Shelley got up and started hunting for her gloves, boots, and hat. "Jane, you have to readjust your thinking. There are no plans! You can do whatever you want. That's what vacations are for."

"I haven't had one for so long I'd forgotten that. Besides, the last couple of vacations I had were with

Steve before he died, and he was a competitive vaca-
tioner. So many miles a day to cover, so many sights
to see, meals mapped out in advance. Up at the crack
of dawn to enjoy—by God!—every minute. Unsched-
uled potty breaks made him wild."

Shelley shuddered dramatically. "If it's not too
crass, may I remind you that Steve is dead and it's a
mercy for a lot of reasons, and besides, this is not
that kind of vacation. Get up whenever you feel like
it. You can have breakfast brought to you, or come
down to the lodge. I suggest the lodge. It's beautiful.
Give me a call when you're stirring. I put my number
on the notepad on the kitchen counter."

"Shelley! You said that word again! Kitchen!"

"Sorry. See you tomorrow."

Jane sat for a while, staring at the dying embers of
the fire. The wine, the cheese, the warmth of the fire,
the comfort of the deep chair—it was all too good to
be true. She finally forced herself to get up and stag-
ger to the bedroom. The girls, to her surprise, had actually turned out their lights and seemed to be asleep,
although she wondered, from the smell as she looked
in on them, if maybe they'd just succumbed to nail
polish fumes.

She had dumped her belongings on the bed nearest
the door, so she tumbled into the one closest to the
glass doors—which she decided was probably the
most comfortable bed in the Western Hemisphere.
She dreamed briefly about Abe Lincoln riding a
moose before she fell into a deep, dreamless sleep.

When Jane finally awoke, she was on her side, facing the glass doors, and for a moment she thought she was dreaming herself into a calendar picture. Blinking, she sat up and gazed in awe. Through the glass doors, beyond the deck, there was a cloudless sky of a pure, clear azure no artist could get away with, and a spectacular rugged, white-crowned mountain peak framed by nearby snow-laden pines. A fat squirrel with tufts on its ears that made it look like a cross between a squirrel and a rabbit sat on the rail of the deck, unabashedly posing. Jane went to the doors and stood mesmerized for long moments. Willard woofed halfheartedly at the squirrel before laying his big head down and going back to sleep.

Jane bathed hurriedly and dressed in the warm clothes she'd brought along—thermal underwear, heavy socks, corduroy slacks, and a flannel shirt with a turtleneck underneath. "I'm a mountain woman, Willard," she said, giving him a gentle prod with her toe. "An overstuffed, but stylish, yuppie mountain woman."

Williard heaved himself to his feet and ambled along with her as she explored the rest of the house. First she actually entered the dreaded kitchen, found some gourmet coffee Shelley had left, and started the coffeemaker. Then she donned coat, gloves, and boots and took the big dog outside. While he visited a patch of ground under a trio of pines where the snow was only halfway up his legs instead of clear to his belly, she stood sucking in lungfuls of thin, cold, snow-and-woods-scented air. It smelled so good she wished she could drink it. Or warm it up and bathe in it.

She took Willard back in, fed him from the bag of his dry food she'd brought along, and gave him a big bowl of water. By that time her coffee was done and she poured a huge mug before dialing Shelley's number. Shelley's first words were, "Did the view knock your socks off when you woke up?"

"I'll say!"

"I was afraid you might close the curtains before you went to sleep and ruin the surprise. I'll be right over."

She was there in a matter of moments, dressed in an aqua ski outfit that made her eyes look the same color, even though Jane knew perfectly well it was an illusion. Shelley was great at fashion illusions.

"I've been exploring," Jane said. "And I'm amazed. This is really some place you could just move into and live in. There are jigsaw puzzles in the cabinets over there. And extra blankets and pillows and even a vacuum and cleaning supplies, besides the extra boots and mittens, in the closet by the front door." She paused warily. "This doesn't mean any-body expects me to clean, does it?"

"No. But normally there isn't any daily maid ser-vice. The units are only cleaned thoroughly between guests. Of course, we're an exception because they're trying to sell us on the place and we're getting the VIP treatment."

"I'd guess, though, that the real cream in the fridge is your doing."

Just then the girls stumbled into the living room, sleep-stupid but eager. "Mom! Isn't this place great?" Katie asked, running a set of mauve-taloned fingers through her tangled hair.

Shelley's daughter, Denise, forgot for a moment that she was a teenager and not only sat down next to her mother, but leaned into a hug.

"It's wonderful, Katie. What are you girls doing today? Trying out for parts in a horror movie?"

"Huh?"

"Your fingernails," Jane explained.

Katie held her hands out and stared at them as if they didn't belong to her. "Euuw, gross! Fungus city!"

"We met this ski instructor yesterday—" Denise said.

They both squealed in ecstasy.

"He said he'd give us a lesson if we'd come over there," Katie continued.

"Where is over there?" Jane asked.

"Down the road. We take the shuttle. Nobody even has to drive us. We just need lift tickets and money for ski rental and boots and poles and lunch—"

"About ten dollars, then?" Jane asked.

"Ten dollars! Mom!"

Shelley intervened. "Girls, everything you want to do here is free and there's lots to do. Starting with breakfast. Go get dressed and you can come down to the lodge with us." When they'd gone, she said, "I saw the ski instructor in question yesterday. He's a thirty-five-year-old lech."

"His age and 'lechiness' weren't even an issue. If Katie's going to break any limbs, she's going to have to find a cheaper way to do it. I was glancing at some ads in the airport while Mel was looking around for what the airline had done with Willard. The prices for lift tickets and equipment rental were astonishing. Oh, Shelley, do we really ever have to go home?" She strolled over to the living room windows and gazed out. "This place is beautiful."

"It is, isn't it?"

Jane drew back, startled. "Oh, it's a cat! I thought it was a big snowball come to life!" A large white cat was sitting on the woodpile at the end of the deck outside. It turned and stared, green-eyed and smug, at Jane for moment, then hopped over the rail and out of sight.

There was a skier sweeping gracefully down the slight incline exposed between the trees. The blue sky, the green-black pines, the shimmering brilliance of the snow, and the skier's crimson pants and jacket created a breathtaking palette of color. As Jane watched, the skier came to a stop, put his (or was it a woman's?) hands on hips for a minute, then held up a pair of binoculars and took a look around.

"It reminds me of Switzerland," Jane said. "My sister, Marty, and I went to a boarding school there once for a semester. Of course, we were just dumb kids and didn't care about the scenery—only about the ski instructors, come to think of it. But even we came out of our haze of hormones once in a while and noticed that it was spectacular."

"What were you two doing in a boarding school?

I thought your parents always took you with them on their postings."

"They did, but my dad was on a stint in some particularly unstable little Balkan country—Holnagrad. Hole in the Ground, we used to call it."

"Holnagrad!" Shelley exclaimed.

"What? You've heard of it?"

"Just yesterday. That's where the historical-society people here are from. Well, not exactly directly from, but their ancestors were."

"The historical—oh, Abe Lincoln and crowd. Are the girls making any progress? I'm starving."

After trying unsuccessfully to hurry their daughters, Shelley and Jane gave up waiting and went ahead. Although it was some distance to the lodge by road, there was a shoveled path running behind the cabins and alongside a crystal-clear stream. The path cut directly through the woods and came out behind the main building. Jane had only seen the front entrance the evening before and was astonished that daylight revealed a very large, sprawling building. The exterior was rough, of large logs and cedar shingles, but banks of spotless windows glittered in the sunlight. Rustic-chic, Jane would have called it if forced to sum up the style.

"There are all sorts of meeting rooms in that wing. There's even computer hookups, modems, and a mini-travel-agency service," Shelley said, acting the tour guide. "At the end is a really elegant restaurant that overlooks the lake this little stream runs into. In the central section there's an indoor pool, an outdoor pool for summer use, saunas, exercise rooms—no, don't panic, nobody's going to make you exercise—a casual restaurant, where we're headed, and a beauty shop. The wing that goes down the hill in stair-step fashion—you can't see much of it from here—has shops, game rooms, a library and a bookstore and I don't know what all else."

They entered through a door by the outside pool, passed alongside the indoor pool, where a few alarmingly healthy individuals were doing morning laps, and emerged into the central lobby just as Mel and the boys entered from the front.

"Jane! You're up," Mel said, surprised. "I thought you'd want to sleep in."

Her sons, Mike the senior in high school and Todd the middle schooler, greeted her and asked for money for the video games. John Nowack, a year younger than Todd, nagged his mother for the same.

"You're not eating breakfast?" Jane asked in amazement. To her, a real breakfast was one of the primary reasons for going on vacation. Naturally, human beings who preferred cold, sugared cereals that pretended to be fun and had never cooked bacon in the morning for themselves wouldn't value the experience quite as much.

"Aw, Mom, we ate hours ago!"

Mel explained that this meant Twinkies and a gallon of milk fifteen minutes earlier. "Jane, do you mind if I take Mike skiing today?"

"I'd be glad for you to." He and her son had always had a cordial, if slightly uneasy, relationship. "It's everybody's vacation to do whatever they like. Well, except for Katie and Denise, who would like to spend a thousand dollars a day and have no restrictions at all."

"As long as you put it that way, I'll pass on breakfast so we can get going right away."

Mel went off to find Mike as Shelley and Jane went into the restaurant. There was a breakfast buffet with every imaginable food, including quite a few Jane couldn't identify but suspected were fruits more prized for their exotic origins than for their taste. A handsome, dark-haired young man who looked like an American Indian stood at the end of the buffet table, making omelets to each diner's specifications. Jane indulged herself in an omelet that involved cheese, mushrooms, artichoke hearts, and crumbled bacon. "I'm trying for a cholesterol prize," she told Shelley as she dug in. "There's a bowl of butter over there that I'm going to slather on myself when I'm through eating."

Shelley, who had chosen sausages and corn fritters with a thick coating of powdered sugar, smiled and said, "Just think, only a few hours until lunch. At least we're uphill from Chicago. We can tuck in our arms and legs and somebody can just roll us home."

They were sitting back, having a second cup of coffee each, when a man approached their table. He was tall, thin, in his sixties, and had the apricot-colored hair that real redheads get when they start going gray. "Excuse me, is either of you ladies Mrs. Nowack?"

"I am," Shelley answered.

"I have a message for you," he said, handing her a slip of paper on hotel stationery.

Shelley glanced at it. "Just my husband saying where he'll be for the morning. Thanks very much. Are you a hotel employee?"

The man laughed, showing a lot of unusually good teeth. "An old geezer like me? No, I'm retired, I'm glad to say. I'm a guest. I was just coming by the

front desk and poor Tenny looked so harassed at trying to get all the accountants checked out that I asked
if there was anything I could do to help her. Those
people check over their bills very carefully, let me
tell you. She was looking for you, so I volunteered to
find you."

"How nice of you, Mr. . . . ?"

"Lucky Lucke. Dr. Ronald Lucke, in my previous
downtrodden life. But everybody calls me Lucky."

"Will you join us for a bit, Lucky? I'm Shelley,
and this is my friend Jane Jeffry. How are you enjoying your stay here?" she asked, answering Jane's silent question as to why Shelley was "taking up" with
strangers. She was being the wife of a potential investor.

"It's a wonderful place. Lots of space for our
meetings. Terrific food."

"Don't you mind having to go elsewhere to ski?"

"Not me. They've got that little bunny slope out
back and that's all the skiing I'd ever want. I've
never broken a bone in my life and I don't intend to
start now."

"I hope you don't get called out of retirement and
are asked to set somebody else's bones while you're
here," Jane said.

"Wouldn't do much good to ask me to. I was a
dentist," he said, grinning. "Are you ladies here for
the skiing?"

They both laughed. "No, we aren't into exercise,"
Shelley said. "We're just along for a break. My husband is here looking into some investments."

"Ah, one of the people thinking of buying Bill out,
huh?"

Shelley looked stricken. "Oh, dear. I didn't mean

to be indiscreet. Mr. Smith is the owner of this resort," she explained to Jane.

"No, no. You didn't let any cats out of any bags," Lucky assured her. "It's just that I know Bill Smith and know he's real anxious to sell out so he can retire to Florida. He and Joanna have a bungalow and a nice boat down there already."

"So you're here because you're a friend of the owner?" Jane asked. "How nice."

"Well, in a manner of speaking, I guess you could say that."

At their questioning looks, he elaborated. "You see, I'm the current president of the Holnagrad Society. Uh-oh. I can see from the way you drew back at the word that you've met our Doris. I'm right, aren't I?"

"Your Doris being the very tall, severe-looking woman?" Shelley asked uneasily.

"Looks like Lincoln? Yup. That's Doris Schmidtheiser."

"Yes, we met yesterday."

"Well, we're here and we all know Bill because Doris has a bee in her bonnet about him."

"Oh?" Jane said politely.

"Yup. The way Doris figures it, Bill Smith is the rightful Tsar of Russia."

—— 3 ——

Jane nearly spewed coffee all over the table.

When she'd recovered herself, she gasped, "I'm sorry. It just struck me as funny. Bill Smith, Tsar of all the Russias. Somehow it doesn't sound quite right."

Lucky laughed. "It doesn't sound much better to Bill, I can tell you."

"Mr. Smith doesn't want to be Tsar?" Shelley asked, smiling. "I guess I can see why. Look at what happened to the last one. I'm sorry. That was a grim thing to say. How did Mrs. Sm—"

"Schmidtheiser," Lucky said.

"How did Mrs. Schmidtheiser come up with this theory?"

"Well, you've kinda got to understand about the Holnagrad Society to start with. Holnagrad's a little speck of a place in the Balkans. Russia had already gobbled it up before World War One. Most of our ancestors fled the country then. And another mob came over during and just after the Second World War. There weren't a lot of people there to begin with and most of them fetched up in the U.S. So the Society was formed in the 1920s to keep traditions alive from the Old Country. You know—dances, songs, language, history. Anyhow, an important function of the

21

Society is the concern with genealogy, and all these
years we've been trying to get church records and
cemetery records and the like out to help trace our
roots. Every now and then somebody'd get a visa to
go back—for a long time the country was behind the
Iron Curtain—and would smuggle out some more
copies of original documents. All very cloak-and-
dagger, with hidden cameras and sneaking into
churches in the dark. Sorry, I'm telling you a lot
more than you wanted to know. Anyhow, when the
Soviet Union fell apart, lots of records were suddenly
available and Doris got her teeth into some."

"Did she go there?" Shelley asked.

"No, but another member of our group did, and
Doris was helping her translate and catalog documents. Doris is a whiz at reading old handwriting.
Don't know how much you ladies know about history, but Tsar Nicholas abdicated and his younger
brother Michael refused the crown. On their own behalf and that of their children. The next in line . . ."
He paused. "Well, the next in line—according to one
theory, let's say—was a cousin of Nicholas and Michael's who was married to a woman from
Holnagrad—a princess. This Romanov cousin saw
which way the wind was blowing even before Nicholas abdicated, and he—the cousin, that is—dropped
out of sight. A lot of people figured he went to
Holnagrad to hide out with his wife's people. But nobody's ever proved it."

"But Doris found something that did prove it?"
Jane asked.

Lucky moved his hand in a "so-so" motion.
"Maybe. She found some church records that seemed
to be of the same family, but they were calling them-

selves Romanofsky. This Romanofsky, the Tsar's cousin—if he *was* the Tsar's cousin at all—died in Holnagrad in 1916 or so—Spanish flu, I think. Doris pieced this together with a ship manifest dated six months later. The ship left Paris, or maybe Lisbon, I don't recall which. On it was a woman calling herself Elsa Roman and her son, Gregor. The Holnagrad princess was named Elsa and their son was named Gregor, so Doris could be right. But there's no proof at all."

"How does all this tie up with Mr. Smith?" Shelley asked, waving at a passing waiter to get some more coffee.

"The ship docked in New York. And just a few months later, in the archives of a Brooklyn, New York, court jurisdiction, a record appeared of a Gregory Ruman or Roman—the handwriting's terrible on the original document—applying for American citizenship and changing his name to Gregory Smith."

"Ah! A Smith at last," Jane said. "But there are a lot of Smiths."

Lucky nodded. "Exactly so. It wouldn't take a genius to come to this country and figure out that the best way to get 'lost' would be to call yourself Smith. And a lot of people have come here wanting or needing desperately to get lost. Anyhow, now workin' back the other way, Bill Smith's father was named Gregory. He was an old mountain man out here, turned up in the early 1920s, and was supposed to speak Russian."

He raised his forefingers and tilted them toward each other. "So Doris worked up one line and down another and figures they match up and are the same person."

"But Mr. Smith doesn't buy it?" Shelley asked.

Lucky shrugged. "Bill doesn't really say much except that he's not interested. He's not much of a talker about anything. All he wants to do is sell this place and retire to Florida."

"And you don't think it's true, either?" Jane asked.

"Oh, it might be true. I don't know. But Doris hasn't got proof, just suppositions. I used to do some forensic stuff. You know, identifying teeth of bodies the police found and such. And I know from that experience that just because something *could* be doesn't mean it *is*. And genealogy's a lot the same. Not quite as exact—it's not a science, after all—but you need more proof than coincidence. And this is a pretty long string of feeble coincidences."

"But how *could* you prove something like that?" Jane asked. "I mean, if you really wanted to—or needed to for some reason."

"Mainly by piling up evidence. And lots of times you can't ever absolutely prove family relationships. But if you have somebody named—oh, let's say Weirather, or something very distinct—and you know the first child of the couple was born in 1859 in Iowa, and you find a Weirather with a one-year-old child in the 1860 Iowa census with the same name as the person you know is your ancestor, and there's nobody else in the whole state with that name—well, it's not precisely proof, but it's a good indication that it's ninety-nine percent certain they're the same person. It is circumstantial, but it's a starting point. Then you can look up your Weirathers in church docu-

ments in that town and start really building your case
with other evidence."

"But with a weird name like that, it makes sense,"
Jane said.

"You know, it's only in the last fifty years or so
that we've gone crazy with forms and documents.
Even at the beginning of this century, a whole lot of
people were barely literate. They could write their
name and do enough ciphering to pay their bills. But
even names were changed pretty often. My own ancestors spelled their name L-U-C-K-E, like I do. But
they also spelled it L-O-O-K-E and L-O-U-K and
L-O-O-C and about a half-dozen other ways. Then
the census takers came around and heard what they
wanted to hear, and they spelled it L-U-T-E and
L-O-O-D. Sorry, I'm on one of my hobbyhorses
again. I've forgotten what you even asked."

"So have I," Jane said, "but it's interesting anyway."

"Anyhow, that's why we have our meetings here.
Bill isn't interested in being Doris's Tsar, but his
nephew Pete encourages Doris and got us to meet
here about four years ago for our annual meeting.
The place, completely apart from the connection with
Bill, suited our needs down to the ground, so we keep
coming back."

"You don't think it's sort of hard to get to?" Jane
asked, remembering the long, dark drive up the
mountains the night before.

"Well, we plan for that. Of course, a lot of people
at the conference are local—we sponsor all sorts of
general genealogy classes at our conference and a lot
of people from Colorado come year after year. As far
as the members of the Society go, we book all our

flights to come in around the same time and hire a bus to bring us all up here at once. That *is* sort of a nuisance, but one we're used to. Anybody who has to come in later or earlier can fly to Vail."

"Vail? There's an airport at Vail? That's close, isn't it?"

He did the "so-so" motion again. "As the crow flies, yes. But there's a mountain between here and there that you can't drive over except in the summer with a four-wheel drive. In the winter, you have to backtrack a long way to get from there to here, so we just stick with the Denver airport and the hired bus."

Shelley had been listening with interest. "You have classes open to other people? Any for rank beginners?"

"Sure. You interested?"

"I am. May I sign up this late and sit in on some of your classes?"

"We'd be glad to have you. It's only twenty-five dollars to attend anything and everything you want. A real bargain, if I do say so myself."

While they'd been talking, Jane had gradually become aware of a faint repetitive noise in the background. In the silence following Lucky's last remark, they all became aware of it.

"What's that sound?" Jane asked.

"Probably a radio turned up too loud someplace," Shelley said.

But people on the other side of the restaurant, where the windows faced the front drive, were craning their necks and looking out at something.

Lucky glanced at his watch. "Ladies, I've enjoyed talking to you. You're very polite to let me run off at the mouth this way, but I've got to get going."

"It's been a pleasure," Shelley said. "Thanks again for bringing me my message. I'll probably see you at some of the classes."

As he departed, Shelley and Jane exchanged questioning looks and wordlessly agreed that they had to see what was going on in front. Shelley signed the breakfast tab, left a hefty tip, and they went across the room to an empty table to peer outside.

At first Jane assumed that what she saw was a display of local color that the resort sponsored. A group of people in colorful garb were doing what appeared to be an Indian dance. There were tom-toms, feathers, beads, and lots of glossy black braids flying. But a moment later, she noticed the placards that others were carrying:

SAVE OUR GRAVES.

LET OUR ANCESTORS REST IN PEACE.

DON'T DESECRATE SACRED GROUND.

And the cryptic, NO LIFT.

The diners were mumbling to one another, speculating on the meaning of all this. But no one had any answers. An attractive woman wearing a long skirt, high boots, and a heavy, fringed shawl had been speaking to one of the demonstrators; as she turned away from him, she caught a glimpse of Shelley at the window and raised a hand in greeting. Then she added a "Stay there" sign. At least that was what Jane assumed it meant.

"That's Tenny Garner," Shelley explained to Jane. "The owner's niece. Or rather, his wife's niece, I think."

They returned to their table on the far side of the room, now cleared. The waiter immediately returned and offered more coffee, which they turned down.

While he was trying to talk them into just another half cup, Tenny joined them. She was probably forty years old, with long, streaky, dark blond hair pulled into a loose bun at the back of her neck. She shed her shawl and said to the waiter, "Bring me about a quart, Al, would you please? Shelley, I'm sorry about this. I'm sure it's all because your husband and his group are here, but how he knew about—"

At that moment a young man Jane immediately categorized as a misplaced surfer stormed into the room. His artfully streaked blond hair, California tan, and muscular physique would have been very attractive if it hadn't been for the furious scowl that distorted his features.

"Tenny!" he exclaimed, striding toward their table. "What are they doing? What are you doing about them?"

"They're demonstrating and I'm having some restorative coffee."

"But you can't let them just march around out there!"

"I can't stop them. They have a permit. HawkHunter showed it to me."

"HawkHunter! That—"

"Pete, this is Mrs. Nowack," Tenny said quickly.

That stopped him in his tracks. He gulped, visibly fought for control of his temper, and rearranged his face into a charming, if insincere, smile. "Oh, I'm sorry. I didn't kn—uh—Mrs. Nowack. How very nice to meet you. I hope you and your family and guests are enjoying your stay."

Tenny and Jane launched into introductions. The young man was Pete Andrews, Bill Smith's nephew.

"So you and Tenny are brother and sister?" Jane asked.

"No!" they both said in unison.

"Pete is Bill's nephew," Tenny explained, apparently embarrassed. "I'm Joanna's niece. Aunt Joanna is Uncle Bill's wife. Pete and I are no relation at all."

"But you both work here?" Jane asked.

Pete preened. "I handle all the entertainment aspects of the resort. Tenny handles the housekeeping." His almost-sneer made it clear that entertainment was the difficult, skilled, imaginative job and housekeeping was both easy and beneath notice. Jane and Shelley, who were both "entertainment directors" and "head housekeepers" of their own homes, exchanged quick glances.

Shelley had sat up very straight and was getting her smiting-down-the-enemy look, so Jane quickly said, "I'm sure you both must work awfully hard. It's nice to see a business that involves the whole family. My late husband was part of a family business." Mention of a late husband usually managed to force people to be courteous, she had discovered.

"Oh—uh—that's nice," Pete said. "And it's been nice meeting you both. I have things to—uh—"

"Run along, Pete. Make sure you get all the quarters out of the video games," Tenny said.

He scowled at her and left.

She stared after him. "That wasn't really nice of me," she mused. "There's no sport in getting the best of him. Poor twit." Then, realizing she was with the wife of a potential investor, she said, "But he's really very good at what he does. Having spent all his useless life 'playing,' he knows all about games and leisure pursuits."

"I heard you mention HawkHunter," Jane said. "Is that the same HawkHunter who wrote the book?"

Tenny nodded. " 'Fraid so."

"Book?" Shelley asked. "What book?"

"Oh, Shelley, you remember. We read it in book club about ten years ago. A very good book, but horribly depressing."

"Sounds like most of what we read in that book club. Depressives Anonymous, we used to call it before we finally had the sense to bail out."

Jane chuckled. "I think it was *Ethan Frome* that put us over the edge. This guy's book was just called *HawkHunter*, wasn't it?"

"I, HawkHunter," Tenny corrected her.

"Oh, yes, that's right. Anyway, it was sort of an Indian version of *Roots*. A story of his family from about the fifteen-hundreds up through his own childhood on the reservation. It really was fascinating, but bigoted in its own way. HawkHunter himself claimed not to have a single drop of 'evil' white blood, but virtually all his ancestors had been hideously mistreated by the white man."

"I'm sure that would have stuck in my mind," Shelley said.

"I don't know how you missed reading it," Jane went on. "Actually, I'm making it sound awful, but it was very interesting. Lots of nifty stuff about the history of this country from the Indian viewpoint. It was a big best-seller for months and months."

"So what's this HawkHunter person doing out there?" Shelley asked Tenny.

"Rabble-rousing," Tenny said grimly. "There's a tiny reservation that abuts Uncle Bill's land—only about ten acres where the village and a couple of houses sit—and HawkHunter's convinced a few of the Indians that they're entitled to our poor little squashed-down mountain. It's a stupid, technical thing, but he's a lawyer, you know. Used to finding niggles. The worst of it is, he's trying to spoil the relationship we have with the tribe."

"How's that?" Jane asked.

"Well, we hire lots of them here. They're wonderful workers and we pay them well and it's been a nice working arrangement ever since Uncle Bill started the resort. Back in the old days, when this was just some primitive hunters' cabins, they worked as guides. Then, when he built it up like it is now, he employed about half the tribe in the construction. Our chef is one of them. So are our accountant and our conference planner, as well as most of the waiters and cleaning crew."

"So what do the placards mean? Especially the 'No Lift' one?" Jane asked.

"HawkHunter is claiming the top of our pathetic little mountain is an ancient tribal burial ground. I don't think the tribe ever believed that until he turned up, and there's no proof whatsoever that there's anything buried up there but a few unfortunate chipmunks that got in the way of a rock slide. But HawkHunter has some of the tribe convinced that somebody—Uncle Bill or the investors—is planning to build a ski-lift mechanism at the top. Which is stupid. It's just a silly hill, and nobody would build a ski lift for a bunny slope."

She took a long, appreciative sip of her coffee.

Shelley had been listening politely, but now asked sharply, "What's the legal niggle?"

Tenny smiled. "Don't worry. Your husband and the

other investors know all about it. Uncle Bill hasn't concealed anything from them. There is a sheaf of legal opinions and precedents in the financial packet he had prepared for them."

"I'm sorry, I didn't mean to imply—"

"I know. But even HawkHunter isn't sure enough of himself to file a suit. He just keeps threatening. And considering how easy it is to file a nuisance suit these days, I think that says a lot about how flimsy his reasoning is."

"So what is it he wants?" Jane asked. "What are the threats about?"

"Oh, not much," Tenny said sarcastically. "He just wants Uncle Bill to give the resort to the tribe."

—— 4 ——

"I'm sorry," Tenny said to their questioning looks. "I've really got to get back to work. I left Aunt Joanna at the desk and she's probably knocking things off people's bills left and right. She can't stand the slightest hint of discontent. I really just came in to let you know that there's a big storeroom off the lobby that has all sorts of boots, mufflers, even snow-shoes and sun goggles. If you want to go adventuring but don't have the equipment, feel free to help yourself. It started out as a lost-and-found, but now we just let guests help themselves."

"Thanks. I may take you up on that," Jane said. "Shelley's going to sit in on some of the genealogy stuff this morning, and I'll take a walk."

Tenny left just as Katie and Denise straggled into the dining room. "Jane, I'm going to run to town and get a notebook," Shelley said. "You don't mind my abandoning you for the morning, do you?"

"Shelley! What do I look like, a wallflower? Go. I'm looking forward to being all by myself for a while. Solitude is such a rare commodity that I can't imagine why you're not interested in it, too. Katie, I see your fingernails are back to normal."

Katie and Denise had stopped by her table, but clearly had no intention of sitting with a mother in public. "The polish took forever to get off. That glue is really tough. You weren't waiting for us, were you?" Katie asked, glancing around to see if anybody had noticed them speaking to Jane. Her gaze lingered for a long moment on the handsome omelet chef.

"Don't worry, I'm leaving in a minute."

"Mom, there was the neatest guy in the lobby. And he was just leaving! Isn't that just morbid?" Katie glanced again at the buffet table, and especially at the handsome omelet maker.

"Hideous," Jane agreed. "Fate deals us these blows sometimes. Katie, that young man is working. Don't try to take up his time, or he could get in trouble with his boss."

"What young man?" Katie asked, all offended innocence.

"The one you're staring at."

"Mother!"

"I'm off to explore. I'll be back here at lunchtime. I'd appreciate it if you'd check in with me then, or leave a note at the cabin."

"I'm not a baby!" Katie said, sticking out her lower lip.

"No, but I'm a mother for life."

I can't win, Jane thought wryly as she headed for the lost-and-found. *If I don't pay enough attention, I'm uncaring. If I show too much concern, I'm overbearing.*

The saving factor was that time passes and teenage girls eventually grow up. Her mother had once told her that about the time her daughters got to be nice young women she could actually like, they went away. There were days when Jane felt that that time couldn't come soon enough.

The lost-and-found was an old-fashioned cloak-room just off the entrance to the hotel. She joined another woman who was rummaging among the items on the shallow shelves. Jane had brought along a heavy jacket and a good, warm stocking cap, as well as insulated boots that were cozy but made her walk like a robot. She added a soft wool muffler and a pair of darkly shaded goggles. Fearing her fur-lined leather gloves might not be warm enough, she put on a fat pair of padded mittens over them. She took a quick glance in the mirror on the back of the cloak-room door and decided the look was Pillsbury Doughboy-ish, but practical.

She waddled out the front door of the hotel and began to follow the road back up toward the Eagle's Nest group of cabins, where she would set out from. Unfortunately, as she toiled chubbily up the hill, she met a couple of young women coming down the road. Jane was sweaty and out of breath. They were all spandex, long, easy strides, flowing tresses, and breezy tans. *I don't think I looked twenty-five when I was twenty-five,* Jane thought grouchily. As soon as they were out of sight, she sat down on an artfully fallen tree at the side of the road to catch her breath.

By the time she'd reached the condo, she realized that she'd badly misjudged in the matter of wardrobe. It was cold, but the air was so thin and dry that it didn't feel cold. In fact, when she was in the sun, she felt downright hot in all those layers. She decided to shed several of them before continuing. Patting herself down, she found her room key in her back trouser pocket and let herself into the cabin.

A pretty young woman with glossy black hair in a bun was sitting on the floor.

"I'm sorry, I must have the wrong—" Jane babbled.

The girl rose quickly. "No, no. You must be Mrs. Jeffry. I'm here to clean. I was just petting your dog."

And sure enough, as she got up, she revealed Willard, belly-up, on the rug in front of the fireplace.

"He probably told you he'd been abandoned and that nobody loved him. Right?"

The girl's dark eyes sparkled. "Right. And that he hadn't been fed for four days."

Jane shook her head. "He's such a liar."

"I think he's a big sweetheart. Are you trying to get out of that jacket?"

"Yes. I know it looks more like a seizure of some kind, but the zipper's stuck, I think."

The young woman helped her. Up close, she was stunningly pretty, with high cheekbones, slanted eyes that looked faintly Oriental, and a nose that was merely strong now and would become dignified and possibly even imperious when she was older.

"Thanks! I was beginning to think it was going to take the Jaws of Life to get me out of that jacket."

"You're wearing a whole lot more clothing than you need to, Mrs. Jeffry."

"I discovered that too late. And I'm Jane, by the way."

"I'm Linda Moosefoot."

"You're an Indian."

"Yes, I know."

Jane smiled. "I'm sorry. I should have known that you'd noticed."

"You're trying very hard to figure out if I'm serious about my name, aren't you? It strikes people that way. But within the tribe, it's a common name. My

brother always says we should just be happy it wasn't
Elkballs or Badgerpiss."

"Have I offended you by calling you an Indian?
Do you prefer Native American?"

"Oh, God! No! That's just trendy twaddle in my
opinion. Anybody who's born in this country is a native American as far as I'm concerned. Your people
might have originally come from Ireland or Germany
or wherever and found my people already here, but
only because we'd come over the land bridge from
Siberia before that. Human beings are all immigrants
on this half of the globe."

"Why, that's a fascinating concept," Jane said.

"Not original, I'm afraid. A college professor of
mine said it and I recognized the truth of it."

"Are you in college now?"

Linda had gone to the closet and was unwinding
the vacuum-cleaner cord. "Yes. I'm just helping out
over the semester break. The Smiths are always looking for extra help over the holidays."

"Do you go to college locally?"

"No. Yale, actually."

"That's a long way from home," Jane said.

"In more ways than just geography," Linda replied.
"You know what's best about being back? Nobody
from around here thinks Moosefoot is a weird name.
Everybody's gone to school with a Moosefoot or had
one of the Moosefoot girls as a bridesmaid or employed a Moosefoot to put on their last roof. I'm not
a token anything here. There are people at school
who are forever trying to make me represent an entire
race. Like I'm not entitled to individual habits and
opinions and traits. You know, a professor—a grown

man who should have known better—once said to me, 'I didn't realize Indians were left-handed.' "

Jane laughed. "Boy, do I ever know what you mean! My dad traveled all over the world and took us along. I grew up being told that I was representing my whole country and that if I chewed my braids or didn't clean my fingernails, people would think all American girls were slobs. To my parents' credit, they didn't claim this was fair or right, just a fact of life."

"Lots of facts of life aren't fair, I guess."

"Am I keeping you from your work? I'm sorry. Tell you what. I need an excuse to sit down and get my breath before I trudge off again. Use the time you would have taken doing the girls' room and have a cup of coffee with me, would you? Doing their room would be a waste of time anyhow. They'll trash it again the minute they come back."

"Sounds good to me," Linda said.

When they were settled, Jane on the sofa, Linda back on the floor with Willard, Jane said, "Do you know there's some kind of demonstration going on at the main lodge?"

"Oh, right. Is that today? You mean HawkHunter, don't you?"

"What's it all about?"

"Hmmm, I'm sorry to say I haven't followed it all closely enough to talk with any kind of authority. I've been working here since I started my break. Something about the Flattop."

"The Flattop?"

"The mountain—well, hill really—behind the resort. It's called that. Some of the elders seem to believe it was once a burial ground, I guess. I'd never heard that before, but I don't always pay as much attention to the old stories as I should. Anyway, HawkHunter's a lawyer, you know, and it's part of his contract with the tribe to represent their interests. They're afraid that somebody's going to build a ski lift and disturb the graves up there. When word got out that Bill Smith was at the point of selling the resort, I guess somebody got concerned that the new buyers would do something like that."

"But Mr. Smith wouldn't have?"

"Oh, no. Bill has always been good to the tribe and the tribe's been good to him. He's an old-timer, you know."

"I haven't met him. Is he elderly?"

"He is, but I didn't mean that. I meant in the sense of being an old-fashioned Colorado type. Live and let live. Mind your own business. Don't antagonize your neighbors. Help without asking for thanks. Don't try to reform anybody. It's a very distinct mind-set. Anyway, he has it. And if he'd wanted to build a ski lift and the tribe said there were graves there, he'd have just respected it without question. But nobody knows about some unknown buyer. The tribe's unhappy that Bill's retiring, but nobody would butt into his business."

"But HawkHunter is doing exactly that, isn't he? Butting in, I mean."

"Well, yes, I guess he is."

"Look, Linda, I'll be honest with you. The reason I'm interested is because my friend's husband is one of the investors who are considering buying the resort."

"Oh, I knew that already. But thanks for being up front about it."

"So what does HawkHunter want? What's the point of the demonstration down at the lodge? To scare the investors off?"

"Oh, no, I don't think so. All he wants is something attached to the deed—that's not the term, but you know what I mean—a rider or something that makes any subsequent buyers have to respect the holy significance of the land and not put up buildings or roads there."

"Is that legal?" Jane asked, not mentioning that this simple-sounding request wasn't what Tenny had said HawkHunter wanted.

"Well, I guess it must be. HawkHunter's a lawyer."

"Then why doesn't Mr. Smith add it to the deed? You just said he had a good relationship with the tribe and would respect their feelings."

Linda scratched Willard's ears and made him mumble with pleasure. "You ask good questions and I'm sorry I don't really have the answers. All I know about this is what I've overheard my mom and dad say. I think—but don't quote me on this—I think Bill doesn't believe there are graves up there. And my own guess is that he doesn't think it's fair to bind future owners to anything that the law doesn't already require. That's just based on what I know of him."

"The live-and-let-live, the-less-government-the-better view?" Jane asked.

"Exactly."

"What do you think of HawkHunter? What's he like?" Jane succumbed to the lure of gossiping about celebrities.

"Have you met him?" Linda asked with a grin.

"No."

"Then wait until you do, and ask me again if you need to."

"What in the world do you mean by that?"

"You'll see," Linda said, getting up and taking their empty coffee cups to the kitchen. "Now I really do have to get back to work."

Wearing a good deal less bulky clothing, Jane set out again on her walk. She had a short, pleasant visit with the green-eyed white cat, who prissily picked its way over some crusted snow, arched its back for a quick pet, and meowed dismissal before moving on. Jane couldn't imagine her slothful cats at home getting along in all this snow. She had to shovel a path for them to the back of the yard when it snowed or they wouldn't go out at all.

Jane discovered why the "mountain" was called Flattop as soon as she got a little farther up the road. It looked like a little mountain ridge that some gigantic hand had leveled off. The resort's only ski slope was on the near side. It was a learner slope with a mild, smooth incline. A mob of people, mainly children, were all over it like brightly clad, but very awkward, ants. A rope looped on a line of stakes enabled them to claw their way back up the slope to keep making practice runs. Among the learners, a trio of obvious experts busily gave advice, helped them to their feet, reattached skis, and generally taught the basics of skiing.

Jane, who had once tried to teach a troop of Brownies, including two left-handers, to crochet, was all sympathy for the instructors.

There were benches at the bottom of the slope,

where the winded and discouraged could sit down to recoup. She joined a little clump of them and listened politely as one of the instructors gave some basic information. Skiing, she discovered, sounded a lot easier than it looked. When the bench cleared, Jane waited for a bit, watching. A minute later, one of the instructors (who had, to Jane's certain knowledge, helped the same lanky teenager to her feet five times) came over and sat down to recover his patience.

"Wouldn't it be easier if there were a lift?" she asked.

He looked at her as if she'd lost her mind. "A lift? Here? What for? Half the skill they need to learn is how to get around when it's not an easy downhill slope. Besides, it would cost a fortune to put a lift on a puny little hill like this."

How odd, Jane thought. If a lift on this slope was such a useless idea, what were HawkHunter and his adherents carrying on about? Jane looked up at the hill, and noticed the same red-clad skier she'd seen earlier. He or she, for it was impossible to tell at this distance, was standing still at the very top of the slope, looking down at the resort through binoculars.

"Is there an easier way to get to the top?" Jane asked the instructor.

"Without skis? Oh, sure. See that path leading into the woods? Just follow that."

Jane checked her watch. Ten-thirty. By the time she walked up there to admire the view, it would almost be time for another meal. And walking up there would burn off the calories she needed to get rid of to justify eating again.

Ten minutes later, and not very much farther up the hill, Jane decided that walking halfway up would probably be enough to earn a good lunch. In fact, a third of the way would almost certainly be sufficient.

5

Jane was back at the restaurant at noon, feeling pleasantly tired and very, very hungry. The thin, deliciously cold mountain air was very appetite-provoking. Although the restaurant was starting to fill up with the lunch crowd, there was no sign of Shelley yet. Jane took a table near the windows and ordered a cup of coffee to sip while she waited. The demonstration was over, and the only people out front now were skiers coming in for a midday break. Jane recognized a few of them from the bunny slope.

She glanced around the dining room again and was surprised to discover that HawkHunter and several of the tribe were among the diners. Strange that they'd feel comfortable on "enemy turf." But maybe not. HawkHunter could very well be a guest here. And the tribe, having always been on good terms with the owner, probably felt quite at home in the dining room. There were two young men, one very old one, and a woman at his table, all speaking intently.

HawkHunter was at the natural center of the group's attention. Jane vaguely remembered the picture of him on the dust jacket of his best-selling book. He had looked young and gawky then, as if he hadn't grown into his teeth yet. But that was fifteen years ago or more. Now he was an extremely handsome man in a very rugged way. And Jane was beginning to sense, even from this distance, what Linda Moosefoot had meant about meeting him and forming her own impression. Even from across the room, he exuded genuine, undistilled charisma. His gestures, a tad "actorish" were controlled but effective; his gaze was direct and penetrating, his body language subtle but macho.

Jane's eye was also drawn to the woman with them. She was quite as striking in her own way as he was. She was an Indian woman dressed in what Jane took to be authentic garb—or, more accurately, a stylish interpretation of authentic garb—a beautifully beaded taupe suede dress, high laced leggings/boots, and long midnight-black, glossy braids with beads and feathers woven in. She sat very still and straight, with the group but aloof from it at the same time. Jane guessed she was in her forties, but she could well be much younger or much older. Her features were classically Indian. She wasn't as pretty as Linda Moosefoot, but only because she didn't look as pleasant and happy. This was a woman who didn't look like she had an ounce of humor in her whole body. Her straight, dark eyebrows were drawn into a frown. As Jane watched, the woman said something, then got up to leave. The men at the table instantly rose to their feet.

Jane found this fascinating. It was her understanding that courtesies such as this were a very Western, almost chivalrous or Victorian, tradition. She remembered from HawkHunter's book that although he showed enormous respect for certain women who were his ancestors, there wasn't any sense of his treating women as if they were somehow fragile and due ostentatious courtesy. In fact, the feeling she had from his book was that women were generally regarded as a fairly likable subspecies of humans. She'd have to get a copy of his book and reread it. Perhaps she wasn't remembering it accurately. Still, in the back of her mind she felt sure there had been something about a medicine woman who was treated with great deference. Perhaps this woman was one such person.

While she was idly speculating, she had failed to notice the approach of a woman who could be none other than Doris Schmidtheiser.

"Hello, there," a gravelly voice said.

"Oh!" Jane said, surprised.

"I didn't mean to startle you. Are you one of our attendees?"

"I don't believe so. You're with the Holnagrad Society?"

"Yes. May I join you for a moment?"

Oh, dear. Shelley had warned her, but Jane was trapped. Even if she'd seen the woman coming, there wouldn't have been much she could have done to escape—short of taking a suicidal dive out the window.

"Certainly. I'm free until my friend arrives in a moment," Jane said, glancing at her watch.

Doris introduced herself as the first vice president of the Society and fussed around with her notebooks and folders, extracting a violently pink handout sheet. Jane decided that, close up, Mrs. Schmidtheiser looked more like an amiable horse than like Abe Lincoln in drag. She had a long, angular face with huge teeth and somewhat protruding eyes. Her voice had a neighing quality that emphasized the visual impression.

"I just wanted to make sure you knew about our classes for the public," she said. "We meet here every year to discuss our own concerns, but we also give an enormous number of very reasonably priced lectures to anyone else who wishes to attend. Beginners' tips, tracing Black ancestors, Jewish genealogy, how to access the National Archives, deciphering ship lists, special information on the Soundex, Miracode and census records, customs regarding Declarations of Intent and which courts to look in for them, writing family histories, preservation of documents and photographs . . ."

Jane held up her hand to stem the tide. "Thanks very much. It all sounds very interesting." (And incomprehensible, she thought.) "My friend is taking some of your classes this morning. That's who I'm waiting for."

"Perhaps you'd like to attend our debate this afternoon," Mrs. Schmidtheiser said, undeterred. She was thrashing among her papers again, presumably trying to find an announcement of the debate.

"Debate?"

"Yes, the Holnagrad Society exists to—"

This time Jane interrupted quickly. "I know about the Society. Lucky—Dr. Lucke—explained it this morning."

"Dear, dear Lucky. Such a fine man. Then you know we have a serious interest in Mr. William Smith, the owner of the resort."

"Yes. Do you mean the debate is about him?"

Mrs. Schmidtheiser nodded. "About Mr. Smith and

a pretender back in Holnagrad." She laughed in a contemptuous, whinnying manner.

"A pretender? To the Russian throne, you mean?" Jane felt like an ass even saying the bizarre words.

But Mrs. Schmidtheiser was too deeply into the subject to recognize its inherent absurdity. "Yes. A member of our group mistakenly believes this gentleman in Holnagrad has a better claim to the title of Tsar than our Mr. Smith. Of course, there's a Eurotrash claimant as well, but *nobody* recognizes his claim except his playboy friends. Excuse me," she said, plunging her big, bony hand into her purse and extracting an orange pill bottle. She struggled with the lid for a moment, removed a tiny white pill, and popped it in her mouth, then took a swig of Jane's water to wash it down.

"This member," she went on, apparently unaware of any lapse of manners, "Stu Gortner, has been in contact with this man back in the Old Country and is forever promoting his cause. He and I are going to present our research to the membership. Of course, we're calling it a debate, but it really isn't. It's truly just a conflict between information on my part and foolish, self-serving speculations on his. Apples and oranges," she said, laughing loudly. Several people at nearby tables turned around to stare at the source of this shrill sound. "Apples and oranges," she repeated, as if she'd made up the phrase and was going to get as much mileage out of it as possible.

"It sounds very interesting," Jane lied. "Perhaps I'll attend if I'm free." She hoped Mrs. Schmidtheiser didn't try to pin her down on what else she had to do at a resort.

Mrs. Schmidtheiser clapped her big hands together

in a gesture that would have been embarrassing if done by a prettier, more feminine woman and verged on the criminal in her case. "Oh, you absolutely must. It's going to be a rousing good time."

Apparently she had complete confidence in her view prevailing.

"I'm sure you're right," Jane said, glancing at her watch again as if she had a very busy schedule and hoping the genealogist would take the hint.

But hints were beyond Mrs. Schmidtheiser. "It's sad, really."

"What is?"

"That so many would be taken in by Stu Gortner. He's a P.R. man, you know." Her voice dripped with disgust. She might as well have been saying he was a known child molester.

"Oh, I see," Jane said weakly. *How would I KNOW this?* she wondered.

"Well, you know the sort." Doris was plunging on. "There's something in it for him. You can bet your bottom dollar on that! It's contrary to the whole purpose and traditional ethics of genealogy. You never start out to prove a particular point, but rather to immerse yourself in the research and let it guide you to the truth. Not that Stu Gortner is the only one to be misled. Alex Haley, of course, is a prime example. He dabbled in order to write a book. His research was the shabbiest thing. Great sloppy leaps of imagination, terrible documentation, all leading to downright falsehoods. It was a disgrace, but then, he did get a lot of people interested in genealogy. We must give him credit there. It wasn't his aim, but it was the result. Genealogy is the fastest-growing hobby in the world, you know."

Jane's head was spinning. She'd never quite known anyone to leap so capriciously from subject to subject and fling around so much casual slander and so many unsubstantiated claims along the way. Jane was beginning to appreciate what a really nice man Dr. Lucke must be to have described this woman so mildly. Most people who had to spend much time around her probably foamed at the mouth at the very mention of her name.

"Excuse me," Jane said. "I believe I saw my friend out there in the lobby, looking lost. Thank you for the information." With that, she snatched up the pink sheet and her purse and leaped to her feet. She had sprinted across the restaurant and out the door before Mrs. Schmidtheiser could even say good-bye.

She all but ran to the lost-and-found room, the only place she knew of to hide. After a few minutes, she cautiously peeked out. Shelley, chatting with Tenny Garner at the front desk, saw her. Shelley spoke to Tenny and pointed at Jane. They both laughed. Jane crept out and approached them. "You're laughing at me?"

"*With* you, Jane. Not at you," Shelley specified. "My guess is that Mrs. Schmidtheiser got you."

"The woman's a menace!" Jane exclaimed. "By my estimate, she can libel one person every forty-five seconds without even breaking into a sweat. Appalling!"

"She probably tried to get you to come to her debate, didn't she?" Tenny asked.

"Oh, yes."

"Poor old thing. I know better than most how annoying she can be. She's a snoop and a nuisance, and I wish Pete would quit encouraging her and she'd leave poor Uncle Bill alone. But for all that, I think she's going to really regret this debate. Stu Gortner will destroy her," Tenny added.

"Why? Is she that wrong? Or is he—God forbid!—even nastier than she is?"

"No, no. He's not nasty at all. That's why he'll win. He's as smooth as silk. A very accomplished speaker. The kind you go away believing without even knowing what he said. He's even talked *me* into deleting charges from his bill, and that's not easy. Poor old Doris will just get red in the face, pop her heart pills, and get nastier and more outrageous until she's alienated everybody in the room."

"Surely the Society doesn't promote this debate," Jane said.

"Oh, no. Lucky says Mrs. Schmidtheiser set it all up without even consulting with him. I thought she was speaking for the group when she reserved the room, and by the time I found out different and talked to Lucky, it was too late. She'd had all her flyers printed up and everything. I think Lucky believes it may teach her a lesson to let her go ahead with this."

"I'm not sure people like that are capable of being taught lessons," Jane remarked.

Tenny turned her attention to a guest who had approached the front desk with a handful of maps and a desperately confused expression.

Jane and Shelley went back to the restaurant.

The table Jane had staked out and then abandoned had been taken, but they found the last free table in the far back corner of the room. As they wound their way toward it, they saw Doris Schmidtheiser at HawkHunter's table.

His other companions had either already left or been driven away by her. She was rattling along, gesturing wildly, riffling through her file folders. HawkHunter, his charisma briefly on hold, was looking frantic. Jane smiled. Nobody was immune from Doris Schmidtheiser's attentions.

They sat down and Jane quickly flipped open the luncheon menu. "I've discovered that this resort is missing only one thing," she said.

Shelley was surprised. "I can't imagine what that is."

Jane grinned over the top of the menu. "Bathroom scales. Shall we order?"

6

After they'd ordered, Shelley got out her small note-book. "Jane, that was a fascinating morning. You won't believe what I've learned. You know I've been meaning to get busy for a year or so on a family history. My mother keeps nagging me to organize all those notes and pictures and old newspaper clippings and obituaries from my grandfather's attic. But I had no idea how to go about it. Now I think I've got a fix on it. It all comes down to the Mormons."

"Mormons? Your family was Mormon?"

"Church of Jesus Christ of Latter-Day Saints, to be more accurate. No, my family wasn't Mormon, but it's the Mormons who have all the information."

"How so?"

"Well, I'm not sure I've got this exactly right, but it seems that according to their beliefs, family ties are forever. When you go to heaven, you'll be reunited with your entire family. All your ancestors. But to prepare for that, you have to know who they all were. So one of the important aspects of belonging to the church is to do your own family genealogy. Knowing your ancestors is part of the religion, you see. Then, when you've got them all sorted out, you submit them somehow to the main church in Salt Lake City

for something called 'sealing,' and then they'll be
waiting for you in the afterlife."

"Okay, but what has that got to do with *your* family?"

"It's like this—since this is a church belief, the
church collects records to make it possible to do this
genealogical searching. Unimaginable numbers and
kinds of records from all over the world. Census records
and family histories and court records from every
county in the country, and church records from
every church that will allow its records to be photographed."

"Oh, not just Mormon churches?"

"No, all kinds of churches. Some of the records go
back hundreds and hundreds of years, and they're all
microfilmed."

"I still don't see—"

"Even though they collect this material for their
own people, they make it available for free to anybody
who wants to use it."

"You're kidding!"

"Not a bit. There are hundreds of Mormon
churches around the country with what are called"—
she paused, checking her notes— "Family History
Libraries. I got a list of them and there's one right in
our neighborhood, in fact. The actual films aren't
there, but the indexes are. You can go in—for free,
mind you—and look through the indexes to all these
documents and learn what film numbers they're on;
then you order the film from where they're all kept in
Salt Lake City. You just pay a couple of dollars for
the postage and handling, and a few weeks later, your
film arrives and you can read it right there on special

microfilm-reading machines at the local church library."

"This is amazing. Who'd have thought?" Jane said.

"Oh, there's more. They've sort of 'distilled' a lot of the basic information down into a couple of gigantic computer programs called . . . let's see . . ." She thumbed through a few pages. "The Ancestral File and the International Genealogical Index. And you can use their computer to get into all this material as well. The example they gave in the class was that if you know your grandfather's name was James Johnson and he was born in 1899, somewhere in the United States, you can plug all that in and the computer will turn out a list of every James Johnson born in 1899 in the United States. Well, not every one, but all the ones they've got in their records so far. Then you can sort through and learn more about each of them to see if one of them is yours. And if one is, you can sometimes find out what film number has original documents about him and maybe who else is researching the same family. That way you could get in touch with some third or fourth cousin you didn't even know about and compare notes on the whole family."

The waiter arrived with their orders: a tuna salad sandwich for Shelley that gave new meaning to the concept of tuna, and a chicken Caesar salad for Jane that was large enough to feed a family of four. They ate for a few minutes in blissful silence. Jane finally took the edge off her hunger well enough to pause and say, "So if you need to look up something—a will, for instance—in some little county in Oregon or some place, you don't have to actually go there and search for it. You can just order a film of the records?"

"That's how I understand it," Shelley said. "The

instructor kept emphasizing that not all records for any given place have been filmed, but hundreds of thousands, if not millions, have been. If you live near Salt Lake City, you can just go into the main library and search without waiting for the film to be delivered. So if you needed something in a hurry, or if you didn't know enough about court jurisdictions to know exactly where to look, you could hire a genealogist there to look it up for you."

"This really is astonishing," Jane said, applying herself to her salad again. "This main library must be a stupendous size. And think of the organization required to keep it operating smoothly. So what else did you learn about?"

"Mainly not to take spelling seriously. Like Lucky was saying this morning, spelling has been pretty haphazard until quite recently. My own guess would be that it didn't get to be awfully important in this country until Social Security. Did you know that most states didn't even have such things as birth certificates until this century? And some didn't require them until the 1930s or so."

"Well, I suppose there were still a lot of people outside cities having babies at home until then. Look over there, Shelley."

Doris Schmidtheiser had moved to another table and was talking with overbearing animation to an older couple. The woman sitting there was frantically signaling for their bill so they could escape if they got a chance, and the man was leaning back in his chair looking stunned by the sheer force of Doris's insistence.

"Poor things. Makes you feel we ought to rescue them, doesn't it?" Shelley said.

"No. Nobody rescued me. Least of all my best friend—who had the nerve to laugh at me when I took cover."

"She's probably trying to get people to come to her debate," Shelley said, ignoring Jane's accusation. "I do sort of feel sorry for her. Maybe I'll go. Just sit in on it long enough to swell the crowd a bit."

"What do you anticipate in the way of a crowd? Two or three misguided martyrs?"

"Oh, she might get a good turnout. After all, this whole Tsar thing is of interest to the people attending the convention. The Holnagradians, or whatever you'd call them."

"I think it's a swell idea for you to offer yourself up that way."

"You're not curious?"

"Not in the least," Jane said. "With my three kids, I've heard very nearly every subject on earth debated at some time or another. Though I'll bet this crowd won't sprinkle their arguments with terms like 'butt breath.' That's very popular just now."

Shelley laughed. "Might liven things up a bit if they did. So what are you going to do instead?"

"First I'm going to find the girls. They were supposed to check in with me—"

"Oh, I forgot. They came by the front desk while you were cravenly hiding in that oversized closet. They said they were going to take ski lessons this afternoon. Here on the bunny slope. And the little boys are still in the game room. They probably won't come out until it's time to go home."

"In that case, the first thing I'm going to do is take a nice, long nap. It's the only thing I'm going to do, matter of fact. I haven't had a serious nap in about

two years. I mean a 'significant' put-on-jammies, get-
under-covers nap."

Shelley signed the tab and Jane took care of the tip.

"Enjoy yourself," Shelley said as they parted ways
in the lobby.

"I am," Jane said. "I really am."

Jane wasn't used to naps and woke up at four feeling
stupid and disconcerted, as if she had a bad case of jet
lag or had suffered a spell of amnesia and lost half a
day. But by the time she'd showered and dressed, she
was feeling quite refreshed. She took Willard out for a
bit of a run and was just coming back when Mike and
Mel showed up. Their faces were sunburned and Mel
was limping along, exhausted.

"Did you have fun? Did you get hurt?" she asked.

"It was great, Mom!" Mike said. "And I did great
for a first-timer."

"He sure did," Mel agreed. "I couldn't believe
how he took to it."

"I met a girl I'm taking out to dinner, Mom, if
that's okay," Mike said.

"Sure. Whatever."

Mike bounded across the parking lot to the men's
quarters. Mel said wearily, "I'm a hundred and four
years old. I could have been beaten with a baseball
bat and feel better than I do now. Do you have any
idea how much work skiing can be?"

"I thought you'd done this before."

"I had. Lots. When I was about Mike's age. Centuries ago."

"Then go take a hot bath and you'll feel better."

"I'd just drown," Mel said grumpily. "Why are
you so damned perky?"

"Perky? Why, Mel, nobody's called me perky in ages. I had a nap."

"A nap," he said, his expression misty and filled with longing.

"Go take one yourself. It's a vacation. You can do whatever you want."

He put his arm around her waist and leered. "Not exactly *anything*. Not on this vacation anyhow, surrounded as we are by your children."

"Well, nearly anything. I'm going to rescue Shelley from the genealogists and see if the boys have suffered any permanent mental disability from a day with the video games. I'll come fetch you later and we'll have a nice dinner, okay?"

Mel agreed and limped off.

By the time Jane found the meeting room where the debate was going on, it was over. Applause spilled out into the hallway as she approached. The door was flung open and Doris Schmidtheiser plunged out, her movements jerky, her big angular face red and working with emotion. Though Jane tried to dodge her, they collided. Papers and folders flew everywhere.

Jane knelt to help Doris pick them up. The older woman muttered tearfully, "I'm sorry. I wasn't looking . . ."

"Quite all right. But I'm afraid you're going to have a time sorting this all out—"

But Doris wasn't listening. She'd grabbed an armload of papers, hoisted herself up and was practically running away.

Jane picked up the rest of the papers, tamped them down, and slipped them into an accordian-type folder Doris had dropped. She'd get them to her later, when

Doris had calmed down. Jane peeked into the doorway and spotted Shelley. She waved a greeting and then got out of the emerging audience's way.

"What a rout," Shelley whispered when she joined Jane in the hallway.

"Mrs. Schmidtheiser ran into me as she came out. She was really upset," Jane said. "What in the world happened in there?"

"Let's go have a glass of wine by the pool," Shelley suggested.

When they were comfortably settled with tall tulip glasses of white wine, Shelley said, "I don't know exactly what happened. Most of the debate was like a foreign language to me. All sorts of sources were flung around. The genealogists, of course, knew the relative merits of them. I didn't have a clue. But it was apparent that Gortner got the best of poor old Doris at every turn. I don't think it was that he had a better case—although I could be wrong—but that he had a more scathing manner and presentation. You know—the kind of thing where you don't present your own side as much as you make fun of everything the other guy says."

Jane nodded. "The kind of thing kids are great at."

"Exactly. It was like watching a pretentiously clever teenager make fun of somebody. It was pathetic. Doris would trot out some document and flash it on the overhead projection screen and go on in a deadly manner for a while. Then Gortner would make some slick, dismissive comment like, 'Surely you're not suggesting that this qualifies as a primary source. . . ?' And the audience would laugh."

"Of course they would," Jane said. "That's a line that always brings the house down."

Shelley shrugged elaborately. "I don't explain 'em, I just report 'em. I have no idea what's funny about that. It was hideous. Poor old Doris. Not that she didn't manage to get in a few slugs of her own."

"What do you mean?"

"Oh, sort of loony, dark allusions to 'enemies within' and that sort of thing. Suggestions that others in the Holnagrad Society weren't all they should be in regard to both the purity of their research and the respect owed her. I got the feeling she was taking digs at Lucky—Dr. Lucke. But I can't be sure. There might be another entire 'party' of people in this thing. Still, her venom was like nothing compared to Gortner's."

"I feel sorry for her, too, but when you promote a bizarre idea you've got to count on a certain amount of flak. And she set this up herself. It's not as if she walked into it as innocently as a lost lamb. Speaking of lost lambs, where are all of ours?"

Shelley looked at her strangely for a moment, then gestured to the pool. "Those two water rats are our sons, and the glamour girls showing off across the way are our daughters. Did you think I chose to sit around the pool because I *like* what humid, chlorine-stinking air does to my hair?"

Jane laughed. "I hadn't even noticed them. Shelley! Don't you see what this means? It's the first hint I've ever had that motherhood is a curable condition!"

—— 7 ——

"Oh, I asked Paul about the deed thing," Shelley said.

"Deed thing?"

"Remember? Tenny said something about HawkHunter wanting Mr. Smith to give the resort to the tribe."

"Oh, right."

"Well, it's actually sort of interesting historical stuff. The tribe did own this land originally. This land and another hundred or so square miles. The government gave it to them, which is bizarre when you consider they were here first and the U.S. government granted them their own land. Anyway, back then, there was a rule that if Indians wanted to sell their land to somebody, they could, but they had to have a Presidential order approving the sale."

"Why?"

"I presume because they didn't have the same concept of land ownership and a lot of people were out to rip them off. Anyway, there was a missionary here at the time, and the tribe wanted to sell him this big chunk where the resort sits now. Of course, it wasn't anything then but uninhabited land. So they all worked it out to everybody's satisfaction and got the President's approval to the sale."

"So what's the problem?"

"The problem was that by the time the document was filed, the missionary was dead. HawkHunter's argument is that the tribe sold the land to the missionary, not to his wife and children. The deed doesn't mention heirs."

"Ah ... I see how that could be tricky. Isn't Paul concerned?"

"No. You see, the President's signature was dated before the minister's death. It just wasn't filed until a week later. That's the most important point. Another is that the tribe accepted payment from the minister's widow, which indicates that they did recognize and approve that the land was going to the heirs. Apparently there have been a number of cases in the last ten years or so with tribes trying to reclaim land, and although some of them have won their suits, the court is obligated to consider intent. Also, the land has had title-insurance all that time, so if by some extraordinarily unlikely chance it came to court and the court ruled in favor of the tribe, the title insurance company would be stuck with the bill."

"So the investors aren't concerned that the tribe has any real legal claim on the land?"

"No, they're not the least concerned about the legalities of the thing. But I think some of them might be very worried about the public relations aspect of it. That demonstration in front this morning was sort of colorful and interesting and lasted only a half hour or so, but if the tribe becomes really militant about all this, it could be bad for the resort's business. It doesn't look good to have stolen land from the Indians and then desecrated their burial ground. Even if neither accusation is really true."

"So Paul and the investors are wavering?"

"Oh, I have no idea how they feel about it. I was just airing my own idea of how they might feel. All they seem interested in is their balance sheets and financial projections."

As she'd been explaining all this, Shelley had glanced around from time to time to make certain they weren't being overheard. Now she gave Jane a subtle end-of-discussion signal as an older couple came into the pool area.

The man went to speak (rather fiercely, it appeared) to the young person who worked at the concession stand where snacks as well as swimming paraphernalia were sold; the woman approached Shelley.

"There you are, Mrs. Nowack. And this must be your friend Mrs. Jeffry!"

"Mrs. Smith, I haven't seen you since just after we arrived. Yes, this is my friend Jane. And you must call me Shelley."

"Oh, good. And I'm Joanna. And my husband's Bill, as you know. Well, well. How are you enjoying your stay? May I join you?"

"Please do," Shelley said.

It would be impossible not to warm to this woman. She was the quintessential grandmother type. Plump, with faintly purple, beauty-shop hair, Joanna Smith even had a big soft bag with her from which she pulled a garish, half-done granny square and proceeded to crochet while they talked. "I hope Tenny's taking good care of you," she said, peering over half glasses that were looped around her neck on a cheap, gilt-painted plastic necklace.

"Wonderful. Yes."

"I knew she would. Tenny is a dear, dear girl. I don't know what we'd do without her. She's my sister's girl, you know. Her father came out here from Tennessee and missed his home. That's why they named her Tennessee, you see. I thought it was an awful thing to do to a child when she was born, but it suits her."

"It is a pretty name," Jane said. "I think it used to be very common to name people for places. My grandmother's best friend was named Philadelphia."

"Is your sister involved with the resort, too?" Shelley asked.

"Oh, no. My poor sister, bless her soul, died when Tenny was just four. She and her husband both. My parents took Tenny in as their own. She was more like a little sister to me. I was only seventeen at the time. Then when I married, I brought Tenny along with me. My folks were in failing health by then, and bringing up a little girl was too much for them. Bill and I never had children—I try to believe that was God's will—and so we raised Tenny."

Jane was doing some mental arithmetic. Tenny looked only about forty, but she could be as much as fifty years old. Which would make Joanna Smith in her early sixties. The same age as Jane's mother. But the difference was amazing. Cecily Grant was trim, fit, and stylish. This woman looked much older. Or perhaps only from a different era. That was it. She wasn't so much old as old-fashioned.

"Is that part of an afghan you're working on?" Jane asked.

"Yes. I'll have to keep it in our own apartments, though. Back in the early days, when it was just hunters who came here, I made things like this for the cabins. But when we rebuilt it as a resort and Tenny took over all the decorating, she told me I had no taste."

"No! I can't imagine Tenny saying a thing like that!" Shelley exclaimed.

Joanna waved her hand deprecatingly. "Oh, but she's quite right, my dear. Tenny has lovely taste. I wouldn't dream of interfering in her decorating. Bill and I are just old frumps. Back when these were just hunters' cabins, we were fine. Bill could talk hunting all day with the guests, and I'd cook plain-cooking dinners for them. Big old roasts and buckets of stew and fried chicken. But when we expanded and made it a resort—well, we were out of our element. Bill was a wonder with the finances, but me and him don't know a thing about skiing or any of that kind of thing. As far as I'm concerned, all this snow is just something you have to put up with. Can't imagine grown people wanting to play in it. And my sort of cooking isn't what appeals to the kind of people who come here." She laughed. "It doesn't even appeal to me anymore. I've gotten used to Tenny's chefs and eating in the dining room. Not sure I even know how to cook anymore. When we retire, I'll have to learn all over again."

"Are you looking forward to retiring?" Jane asked, just to keep the conversation going. "My father keeps talking about retiring, but I think he's scared to death somebody will take him seriously."

"Not us. We're ready. At least Bill is. A place like this is an awful lot of work and worry," she said, blissfully unaware that this wasn't the kind of thing a seller should be saying to a potential buyer's wife. "Every time some pipe bursts in the middle of the night or half the maids come down with the flu at the same time or some group that's booked a big block changes their mind, Bill has to take care of it. Tenny's a big help, but it always comes back to Bill one way or another."

Bill had finished talking to the concession attendant and joined them. He wasn't a big man by any means, but he had a wiry, rugged look. And, as soon became apparent, the manners to match. Joanna introduced him to Jane and he merely grunted noncommittally. "That damned kid thinks he's on vacation or something," he groused.

It took them all a moment to realize he meant the employee he'd just been talking to. "Told him twice to clean the storeroom and it hasn't been done yet. I told Pete it was a mistake to hire a white kid for the job. The Indians work much better. They don't want to yammer around socializing with all the swimmers. They just want to do their job and get paid and go home."

"Now, Bill," Joanna said soothingly, "you know the guests like Tory. They're always saying how nice he is."

" 'Nice' don't get the storeroom cleaned. And what the hell kind of name is Tory, anyway?"

Jane suddenly understood why he'd been so happy with the hunters' cabins and felt the resort was such hard work. The man wasn't suited to it at all. He was a tough, macho, reactionary old buzzard. Still, it had been his own choice, and in his own way he was good at it. At least, he must be for the place to be so nice and successful. Tenny's responsibilities must have extended to keeping him out of the way of the guests. Jane noticed that Joanna had finished a light yellow row on her granny square and had selected a bright neon pink for the next row. Yes, between hiding Joanna's ghastly domestic products and Bill's abrasive personality, Tenny had a full-time job.

As they'd been talking, Jane had been watching Todd and John, who were starting to look like big white raisins with blurry red eyes. She excused herself, got them out of the pool and dried off, and insisted, over their halfhearted protests, that it was time to get dressed and rest for a while. While they were getting ready, she brought them burgers and fries packed in the reusable padded boxes the resort used for carryout orders.

When she came back to the pool, the boys were bundled up and ready to go. She took her leave of Shelley and the owners, saying she needed to dress for dinner, and abandoned Shelley to the Smiths. Shelley wouldn't mind; she was in corporate-wife mode. Jane had tried to get the girls out of the pool, but they were determined to stay and claimed that Tory had told them they could eat dinner at poolside. Jane and the boys walked back to her quarters, taking the shortcut through the woods this time. It had gotten dark quite suddenly and snow was falling, but the path was clear and lighted at five-foot intervals with little lanterns. She reached her door just as Mel did from the other direction.

"You've napped. I can tell," Jane said.

"Sheet creases on my face?"

"No, just bright eyes and a nice smile. Are you ready for dinner?"

"I can't ever remember being hungrier."

"Good. I'll change fast."

"I'll go back and let the boys in and get them set-

tled for the evening," he offered. He returned a few
minutes later and came in and turned on CNN in the
living room while Jane ran a comb through her hair,
put on fresh makeup and some of her new clothes.
Shelley had made her shop before coming on this
trip, and her "best dress" for the resort was a long red
suede skirt that not only had been on sale, but fit her
perfectly. Shopping never went that well for her unless Shelley was along. Bargains of this sort seemed
to call a siren song to Shelley as she stepped over the
threshold of a dress shop. She'd stand for a moment,
head cocked, eyes half closed, then head directly for
the best deal in the store. With the red skirt, Shelley
had selected a cream silk blouse and a sweater/jacket
with the cream of the blouse, the red of the skirt, and
several shades of khaki and brown in a splashy leaf-
like pattern. It was really a stunning outfit.

"Wow!" Mel said, when she reappeared. "You
look great!"

"Shelley picked it all out," Jane admitted. "Let's
go. Oh, I almost forgot again. I've been carrying
around a folder that belongs to one of the genealogy
people."

"Why are you carrying it around?"

Jane explained briefly about the genealogy debate
and how she'd run into Doris Schmidtheiser and
helped pick up her papers, but Doris had fled in mor-
tification before Jane could hand these over. "I just
need to drop them off on the way to dinner. I checked
on where she's staying and it's on our way. I meant
to leave them as I came here, but forgot."

"Okay, but you won't stay and talk, will you? I'm
starving."

"Promise."

Jane's sweater/jacket had a hood that looked warmer than it turned out to be. She was stylish, but freezing by the time they got to Doris's cabin. She had tried to ignore the cold by talking a blue streak about Doris, the Holnagrad Society, and Doris's claim that Bill Smith was the rightful Tsar. When they arrived, Jane tapped lightly on the door and it swung open under her touch. Doris must have been so disconcerted when she returned that she hadn't pushed it closed properly.

"Mrs. Schmidtheiser?" Jane called through the open doorway. "Yoo-hoo! Are you home? Mrs. Schmidtheiser?"

There was no answer.

"I'll just put it inside," Jane said. But the moment she stepped inside she knew something was wrong. "Mel," she said softly.

The alarm in her voice brought him instantly to her side.

The cabin was arranged just like Jane's, with an entry hallway that opened onto the living room straight ahead and the kitchen to the left and the bedroom hallway to the right. In front of them, papers were strewn all over the floor.

"Stay here," Mel said sharply.

He went into the living room and Jane, in spite of his orders, followed him.

Doris Schmidtheiser was crumpled on the floor, next to the coffee table. Mel was kneeling beside her, feeling for a pulse. "Janey, you better wait outside."

"I'll freeze out there," Jane said. "Is she dead?"

"I'm afraid so."

"Heart attack? She took heart pills."

"Probably. I'll call the police, then alert the hotel people about what's happening."

He went to the phone, but pulled out a handkerchief to put in his hand before he picked up the receiver. He dialed 911, spoke briefly, then dialed the hotel operator. "Who's the owner, Jane?" he asked while waiting for the hotel operator to pick up.

"Bill Smith, but I think you probably want to ask for Tenny Garner."

He did, then identified himself and told Tenny that a guest had died and he'd already summoned help.

"Why the handkerchief?" Jane asked after he'd hung up. "If you think it was a heart attack."

"No reason especially. Just habit."

Jane looked at him.

"Well, that and the mess. Whenever you have a death in the midst of this kind of disorder, you have to wonder."

"You think it's murder?"

"No!" he said emphatically. "I don't think any such thing, and don't let your imagination go rocketing off, either. She's an old lady who had a bad afternoon. She had heart troubles and was under a lot of stress at a high altitude. That's it."

"Okay, okay. I was just asking."

Still, she took a quick look around, careful not to touch anything. There was a coffee cup on the low table, nearly empty. Doris was still wearing her outdoor boots, though her coat was nowhere to be seen. Presumably she'd hung it up when she came in. There was a faint odor of overcooked, almost burned coffee in the air, and Jane discovered that the coffeemaker in the kitchen was still on and the coffee had cooked down to a half inch of dregs. She turned it off, fearing nobody else would think of it. Doris's briefcase was upside down on the floor next to her, the papers and folders spread in a messy circle. Jane crept down the hall to the bedroom—this cabin had only one—and it, too, was littered with papers. Several notebooks gaped open, their pages awry as if the contents had been skimmed in a frenzy.

Jane heard a siren and went back to open the front door. A moment later, an ambulance pulled up and medical attendants leaped out and ran in with their equipment. A few seconds behind them was a patrol car. A good ol' boy of a sheriff hoisted himself out of the driver's side, and a rabbity deputy hopped out the other door. The sheriff ignored Jane as he rolled past.

"Excuse me, miss," the deputy said.

"Well, are you the fella who called this in?" the sheriff boomed.

"Mel VanDyne. Yes, I placed the call."

"You a relative?"

"No, I've never seen this woman before. But my friend had some papers to return to her. When we got here, the door was open and we found the body."

"Well, now, ain't that convenient."

Uh-oh, Jane thought.

Mel came into the front hallway. He didn't look pleasant.

"Jane," he said with deadly formality, "I think maybe you better go down to the lodge. I'll join you in a few minutes."

"Mel! Why didn't you tell him you're a detective?" she whispered.

"Because I'm not. Not here and now. I'm on vacation. Go on. I'll be with you shortly."

"Okay. But I'm going to order drinks and appetizers the minute I sit down, so you better hurry."

8

They had dinner reservations in the more formal restaurant. It was an elegant, dimly lighted, artfully arranged room that overlooked the small lake. From her table next to the windows, Jane could watch the skaters below. The table itself was set with superb pink linens, the best-quality restaurant silverware, and beautiful china with a muted pink-and-gray Oriental floral pattern. Although it seemed late to Jane, her internal clock having been completely undone by her earlier nap, the restaurant was just starting to fill up for the evening.

Jane finished her glass of wine and half the appetizers (bite-sized egg rolls with a spicy crab filling). After a while she finished the rest of the appetizers and drank Mel's wine. Then she ordered coffee and nibbled the Italian parsley that had decorated the appetizer plate. Starving, bored senseless, and bursting with curiosity, she couldn't even tell Shelley what had happened, because this was the night Shelley was being hostess to the investors at a cocktail party and dinner in her and Paul's condo.

She studied the other diners for a long while, but decided she was drawing as much attention as she was giving. One middle-aged man with what he no doubt imagined was an attractive two-day beard stub-

74

ble and a lot of gold chains winked at her. *My God! He thinks I'm a hooker!* she thought with horror.

She told the waiter she'd be back and ran to the little magazine-and-book shop next to the front desk, then checked on Katie and Denise, who had finally emerged from the swimming pool and, fully dressed, were eating burgers at a table on the pool apron. Back with something to read, she drank another cup of coffee, then visited the rest room for the second time. Just as she was returning to her table, the waiter approached to tell her there was a phone message that said she was to order two dinners and her companion would be with her in a moment.

After studying the menu one last time—she nearly had it memorized—she ordered two of the more interesting entrées on it: elk stew with cattail pollen dumplings for herself, and a buffalo steak with horseradish/rosemary sauce and blue cornmeal dressing for Mel.

Mel managed to arrive before the meal did.

"What took you so long?" Jane asked.

"The local sheriff is an ass!" he said, sitting down heavily. Jane could hear his stomach rumble. "He was all for just carting off the body and letting your pal Tenny Garner send in a maid to clean up the room."

"And you tried to stop him?"

"Of course I did. That's not the way to treat a sudden death."

"I thought you were the one who said there was nothing suspicious about it."

Mel took a deep breath. "I don't know whether I should tell you this or not—"

"You might as well," she said sweetly. "After all, we're both on vacation. It has nothing to do with us."

He cocked an eyebrow at her and thought for a long moment before finally saying, "Did you notice the 'distribution' of all those papers?"

"Yes; they were everywhere."

"No, they weren't."

"Well, I guess there weren't any in the bathroom or the kitchen."

"That's not what I mean. I'm talking about the living room."

Jane closed her eyes, picturing the room where they had found Doris. Papers all over. On the coffee table, the sofa, the floor . . .

She opened her eyes very wide. "Oh! She wasn't lying on any of them, was she?"

"Bingo."

Their salads arrived. Trendy, rather bitter lettuce with little groupings of berries and slivers of something crunchy like water chestnuts, only pink. Normally Jane would have questioned the waiter about the ingredients, but not tonight. "So you assumed the papers had been flung around after she collapsed."

"It seemed likely. First I suggested that the sheriff have the remains of the coffee in her cup tested, but he said there was no need for that. She was an old lady and just had a heart attack and he, the sheriff, had a houseful of company at home—his in-laws, who were probably drinking all his best beer while he was wasting time, the in-laws being the greedy sort who would do that kind of thing to an absent host. About that time Ms. Garner got there, heard the last of the conversation, went and puttered around the

kitchen and said there was another coffee cup missing."

"Ah—so maybe she was having coffee with somebody who took the other cup away. Fingerprints,
maybe?"

Mel shrugged. "You never know. So the sheriff—
his name is Plunkbucket, by the way—"

"It isn't!"

"No, but it's something like that. He says every
time he's ever been up here, people are roaming
around the grounds with coffee cups and glasses and
things, and Ms. Garner admits that's true and the
missing one might just turn up in the spring melt.
Apparently all sorts of stuff show up when the snow
disappears every spring."

"Didn't you tell him you're a detective?"

"Oh, I did that. And it made the situation about ten
times as bad. He resented me enough before that;
then, when he found out I was not only a detective,
but from Chicago as well, he really got nasty. City
slickers trying to tell him how to do his job, et cet-
era."

"But did he agree to test the coffee left in the
cup?"

"Well, yes and no. He's testing it, but only because
of my threat to report him to anybody I could find to
listen if he didn't."

"You feel that strongly that her death was suspicious?"

"No, I don't. But I was pissed off by then. Some
of her genealogy chums had turned up by that time,
and they were backing him up like mad that it was
just an unfortunate but inevitable result of her bad
heart and a disastrous afternoon. They told him all

about the debate and how she'd been laughed out of the room. What the hell *is* this stuff I'm eating?"

"I dunno. Fruit of some kind. Don't you like it?"

"It's okay. Just a funny texture. I'm hungry enough I'd probably eat broccoli if somebody put it in front of me."

"How did the sheriff explain the papers thrown all over?"

"Just a fit of pique. He actually used those words, I swear. After hearing of the debate that the genealogy people kept yammering about, he figures she came back, fixed herself a cup of coffee, then got herself all worked up to a temper tantrum and threw her work around. This activity leading, naturally, to a heart attack."

"But, according to that scenario, why weren't there any papers under her body?"

"Coincidence," he said. "And the big slob could be right. I told him so. I kept trying to impress on him that I wasn't claiming there was anything suspicious, just trying to convince him there could have been foul play and if he didn't have the scene examined carefully, he might be sorry later."

"So who won?"

"I guess I did. He didn't want to look too bad in front of all the gawkers who'd already come and pawed around, disturbing any evidence that might have been there originally. So he called in some more deputies and started checking the place out properly. Too late, but better than just slamming the book shut on the woman without a second thought."

"You've done your duty, then."

The waiter took away their salad plates, leaving tiny palate-clearing scoops of lime sorbet, then was back shortly with a mystery soup and some little muffins with bits of leaves cooked in them. Spicy apple butter accompanied the muffins. Jane offered hers to Mel, not mentioning that she'd eaten his appetizers, and he wolfed both muffins down.

"I'll probably find an elk head in my bed tonight," he said around half a muffin.

Mel refused to talk any more about Doris. Instead, they concentrated on their dinners. Mel's buffalo steak turned out to be what Jane called Swiss steak—a pounded, slow-cooked meat. The waiter explained that buffalo, though growing in popularity, was a much tougher meat than cow and needed more cooking. Mel claimed it was delicious, but complained that the blue cornmeal dressing tasted blue.

"Tastes blue? What in the world do you mean?" Jane asked, laughing.

"I don't know. Just blue. I've never eaten blue food before. I don't think in the cosmic scheme of things we're meant to. How's your elk stew?"

"It doesn't have much meat in it. It's mostly vegetables and dumplings," Jane said. But after she'd tasted it, she realized why. The elk was a highly flavored meat and any more of it would have been overwhelming. The cattail pollen dumplings, however, were absolutely delicious, with a sweet, nutty taste unlike anything Jane had ever eaten. It was, all in all, an instructive and flavorful meal.

The restaurant was, like most now, nonsmoking. Since Mel didn't smoke and Jane had been quitting in slow motion for over a year and was now down to only a half-dozen cigarettes a day, this didn't bother them, but they were pleasantly surprised when the

waiter invited them to take their dessert and a com-
plimentary after-dinner brandy in the Cigar Room.
This well-screened appendage to the dining room
turned out to be an interesting and attractive room
with excellent ventilation, windows on three sides
looking into deep woods, and small, intimate tables.
There was a dessert trolley that was rolled silently toward them as they took a table near the inside wall.

Jane chose a parfait glass beautifully layered with
raspberries, white chocolate shavings, and cream,
while Mel picked a custard with a caramel-and-
ground-hazelnut topping. Neither of them could finish their desserts. Jane sat back, looking over the
other people in the room. "See that man over there
with the light orange hair?" she said. "That's Dr.
Lucke. Lucky. He's the president or chairman or
whatever of the genealogy group. He's very nice."

"And who's that with him? The slick-looking
one."

"I'm not sure, but he was standing near the podium when I went to the door of the room the debate
was in. I think maybe he's the man who devastated
poor Mrs. Schmidtheiser. Gordon? Gorton? Something like that."

"And in that corner?" Mel asked, tilting his brandy
snifter slightly to indicate where another two men sat
talking seriously.

"Hmmm. That's an interesting combination. The
dark, handsome one is HawkHunter. I'll have to fill
you in on all the Indian business. The funny thing is,
the man with him is Pete Andrews. He's the nephew
of the owner of the resort."

"I thought he was somebody official. He turned up
at Mrs. Schmidtheiser's cabin while the sheriff was

there. He seemed sincerely upset about her death. I guess he would be. Resorts don't like guests dying."

"He actually knew her as well. You know she was promoting Bill Smith as Tsar of Russia. Well, Pete's the nephew who encouraged her and the Holnagrad Society people to come here for their conventions in the first place."

"What do you mean about it being an interesting combination?"

"HawkHunter is giving the owner a lot of trouble, and the only time I met Pete Andrews, he was complaining bitterly—almost hysterically—about Hawk-Hunter. But they look like they're getting along now." She explained briefly about the conflict over the ownership of the land.

She frankly stared for a few minutes. The two were talking seriously, but there was no hint of either cordiality or animosity in their appearances. A waiter hovered near them.

"Mel?"

"Hmmm?" he responded dreamily.

"If her death weren't natural—"

"Jane!"

"No, I'm not suggesting we butt in. I'm just curious. An intellectual exercise. If it weren't natural, why do you think anybody would have done her in? She was obsessive and not terribly likable, but—"

"Jane, I don't know enough about her to speculate and neither do you. More important, I don't want to. I'm on vacation. I've already involved myself a lot more than I should have. It's Sheriff Plumbasket's problem now."

"Plumbasket?"

"Something like that."

"I'll probably find out that his name is Jones," Jane muttered.

"Jane, I wonder if the hotel is full."

"I have no idea. Why?"

"I was just thinking . . . since our rooms and travel and meals are all paid for, this trip is virtually free. Except for tips and things."

"Yes?"

"Well, it seems downright ungrateful not to pay for at least one room. A room where, maybe, you and I could be alone for a few hours." He ran his hand lightly along her forearm.

"I didn't bring along a decent nightgown," she warned him, smiling.

"My only interest in your nightwear is getting you out of it, in case you hadn't noticed."

"I had noticed. And don't think I don't appreciate it. Although I hate to think of the money I've wasted at Victoria's Secret in the last couple months."

Their love life was about as spontaneous as building a pyramid, Mel had sometimes complained, but the complaint wasn't too serious. He'd accepted, with fairly good grace, Jane's "rule" which was that she was simply too bone-deep old-fashioned to conduct an affair in her own house.

"I'm the mommy there," she had told him. "It's not that I imagine my kids don't know the nature of our relationship, but I just couldn't get 'into the spirit' of the thing with them roaming around the house, blabbing on the phone in the next room, or banging on the bedroom door to ask where I put their favorite jeans."

She'd gotten so wholeheartedly "into the spirit" when she was away from home—at his apartment and on the two weekend trips they'd taken—that he'd have been a fool to mess with a good thing.

She hadn't added to her prohibition to lovemaking in her home, *Unless we were married,* because that was a word neither of them wanted to use.

Yet.

Or maybe ever.

"I think you're right," she said. "It would only be polite to pay for a room. Just as a way of thanking our hosts, of course. An entirely unselfish plan."

"I'll see if there's anything available. Wait right here," he said.

Jane watched as he left the room.

"Jane . . . Mrs. Jeffry. Are you alone? Would you like to join us in an after-dinner stroll?"

Dr. Lucke and his dinner companion were standing next to her table.

"Thank you, Lucky, but I'm alone only for the moment. My friend has gone to—to make a phone call," she improvised, wondering if she was blushing, and if so, whether they could tell in the dim lighting.

Lucky introduced the other man as Stu Gortner, the person who, as Jane had guessed earlier, had debated Doris Schmidtheiser that afternoon. As soon as the introductions were done, Gortner begged off the walk idea. "Been a long day. Think I'll turn in," he said with a wink. Jane shuddered. She hated it when men she didn't know winked at her. There was something intimate and creepy about it.

"Ah, well, maybe I'll give it up, too," Lucky said. "And just sit with Jane for a minute. Do you mind?"

"Not a bit," Jane said politely.

When Gortner had gone, Lucky sighed and said,

"I'm sorry. I won't intrude on your evening. I just had to get free of him."

"Why is that?"

Lucky sighed again. "I don't like to talk behind anyone's back, but that man is awful. Just awful. Invited me to dinner, then spent the whole time crowing about what he did to Doris. And poor old Doris dead! You'd think he'd know to show a little respect."

"Oh, you know she's dead? I didn't want to be the one to tell you. Craven of me, I guess."

"Yes, I know. Tenny called me to get some information for the sheriff about her family and who should be notified and such. But even if she hadn't, I'd have heard. Word's gotten around already."

"I didn't get to hear the debate," Jane said. "I understand Mr. Gortner made her look silly."

Lucky nodded. "And he wasn't playing fair, if I can use such a childish term. He's one of those people who tries to win people to his side by ridiculing his opponent."

"So his arguments on behalf of his—uh—candidate weren't better than hers?"

"Hell, no! Excuse me. Heck, no. He didn't present any really convincing evidence at all, just made everything Doris said look foolish. And, bless her heart, Doris could look pretty foolish all by herself without any help."

"Why would he need to do that? Just a naturally competitive spirit?"

"I wondered about that, too. Until tonight. See, part of the reason he invited me to dinner was to ask for the Society's backing on some plans he's got."

"Which are—?"

"See, Stu is an old P.R. man. Made a mint over the years pushing everything from pretzels to presidents of corporations. You wouldn't believe some of the people and things he claims took off like Roman candles because of his publicity. Anyhow, he's really latched onto his candidate, as you put it. He retired two years ago, and when the Iron Curtain came down, he took a trip to Holnagrad and met this guy— Stanislas Romanov."

"Is that really his name?"

Lucky looked at her. "That's a very perceptive question. I wish more people had the brains to ask it. I have no idea."

Jane kept glancing over her shoulder as tactfully as she could. No sign of Mel yet. "So he met Stanislas?"

"Right. Stu says he took up with him just to keep his hand in the business. Sort of like I work one day a week at the free clinic just to keep in touch. But Stu naturally turned his mind to how to make money off this man."

"He's found a way?"

"Has he ever! That's what he was bending my ear about. He's signed himself up as this guy's agent. Says he's very attractive—speaks English with a sexy foreign accent, has great Continental manners. All that. Stu wants to bring him over to this country, get him on TV, sell movie rights and book rights and Lord only knows what else. And he wants us to back him up. Sort of be his cheering section. The nerve!"

"That does sound sleazy. The Society won't go along with it, will they?"

"Not if I have anything to say about it. But Stu knows how to convince people of almost anything.

He's already got a bunch of members in his corner. They say it's a great way to draw attention to our group and its concerns, make people aware of our heritage, enlist new members, all that. 'Course, they're being had. Stu's convinced them he's doing all this for the Society when he's just doing it for himself."

Mel came through the doorway and Lucky stood up suddenly. "I'm sorry for bending your ear like that. Just got a crawful. Have a nice evening."

Oh, I think I probably will, Jane thought.

It wasn't until Jane and Mel were leaving the lodge that she realized she was still carrying around Doris Schmidtheiser's file folder.

9

"Do you know what I liked best?" Jane asked an hour and a half later.

"This?" Mel said, demonstrating. "Or maybe this?"

Jane laughed. "That's not what I meant. What I liked best was that before we came here, you'd already called and made sure the boys were all settled in your place with their dinner and their new Nintendo game."

Only because I knew if I didn't, you would—and possibly at an inopportune time," he said, lazily stroking the curve of her shoulder.

Jane sat up, turned on the bedside light, and started looking around for her clothes. "That's exactly what I *did* mean. That you understand."

"I guess this is leading up to you turning back into Mommy any minute now."

Jane shrugged. "It *is* my job. And unlike you, I don't ever get a vacation. Do you mind horribly?"

"And if I did? Never mind. I don't want to know. I'll fix us some coffee."

"Darn it! I've still got that folder," Jane said, sorting through her things. "Doris Schmidtheiser's. I meant to give it to Lucky and it went right out of my mind when he started talking about that Gortner man."

As Mel walked Jane back to her cabin, she told him about her conversation with Lucky. "He was really shocked by and disgusted with Stu Gortner's attitude."

"And you think that means this Stu person killed Mrs. Schmidtheiser?"

"You're ruining my punch line. No, I don't mean that. But if it turns out that her death wasn't natural, I think he bears looking at. After all, her death removes the main obstacle to his promoting his candidate. Bill certainly isn't going to pursue his claim, and Pete doesn't know enough about genealogy, I don't think, to push it along himself."

"This is too strange to accept, Janey—the whole idea of trying to put somebody back on the throne in Russia."

"Of course it's nuts, but I don't think Stu Gortner has any interest in that angle of it. He just wants an interesting figure to promote as the rightful Tsar without getting involved in actual politics. Sort of a new Anastasia. Somebody had to have made a lot of money out of that poor woman. At least that's what Lucky led me to believe. Gortner just wants a celebrity to make money off of. Lucky talked about book contracts, movie rights and things like that."

"So what difference would Mrs. Schmidtheiser have made in the plan?"

"She was an outspoken fanatic who might well have trailed him around, debunking his guy's claim."

"But, Jane, it's absurd to think anybody would care enough about this to kill someone."

"It's absurd to us. But not to them. And as far as

Stu Gortner is concerned, it's all about money. Maybe a lot of money. Isn't that what most people kill for? When someone is threatening their financial well-being?"

They'd reached her cabin. "We don't know that anybody *was* killed for anything, Janey. And even if she was, it's not our problem to solve. It's what's-his-name's. The sheriff."

"But—"

"But nothing. Say good night, Gracie."

Jane laughed. "Okay, okay. I give up." She rummaged in her purse for her key.

"Where've you been?" Katie asked when her mother came in.

The girls had MTV on, but, knowing Jane's loathing of the station, they switched to a movie channel as soon as she appeared.

"Oh, here and there," Jane said. "Mel and I ate at the fancy restaurant. You wouldn't believe what we had for dinner. Oh, look what movie's starting!"

"Just some old thing," Katie said, glancing over her shoulder.

"Some old thing! That's blasphemy! It's *An Affair to Remember!* Don't tell me you've never seen it."

"Naw, I don't think so."

"Then sit down right now. You can't grow up until you've watched it. You'll love it. Believe me."

Katie and Denise exchanged quick looks that said, *Mothers. What can you do?* and dutifully took their places side by side on the sofa.

"Did I see some microwave popcorn in the kitchen?" Jane asked. "I'll fix us a bunch. And find a box of tissues. You'll need them before it's over."

Two hours later, they all stumbled to bed, weeping happily.

Saturday morning, Jane called Shelley.

"I didn't wake you, did I?"

"No. I was debating about when to call you," Shelley replied.

"How'd your dinner go?"

"Lovely. Tenny arranged it all and the food was fantastic. I called around, trying to find you about nine last night. Where were you?"

"Oh . . . here and there. Want to come over? I've got lots to tell you. Did you know Mrs. Schmidtheiser died last night?"

"No! Oh, how awful. Poor thing. What was it? A heart attack?"

"Maybe so. Maybe not."

"Jane! What do you mean by that?"

"I'll tell you all about it when you get here. Give me about twenty minutes. The girls are going to try skiing, and I told them I'd go over to the bunny slope with them and make sure they had everything they need. Like money, I suspect."

Jane was slightly delayed by Willard. The green-eyed white cat had made another casual appearance on the deck, and this time Willard saw it and went berserk. When she took him outside a few minutes later, he was determined to find the cat and, as he was on a leash, dragged Jane all over the woods before she managed to haul him back inside. But she and the girls finally got on their way.

It had snowed again overnight, and there hadn't been enough skiers yet to mess up the pristine sweep of the slope. A few hearty souls had already trudged

up the hill, making a sloppy herringbone pattern with
their skis and wobbling tracks coming back down.
The three instructors were helping others get ready to
ski. Jane sat down on a bench at the bottom of the
slope and waited patiently as the instructor showed
the girls how the skis attached to their boots, demonstrated a few basics, and sent them up the hill.

Jane told the devastatingly handsome young instructor her name and room number, just in case one
of the girls broke a leg or something.

"Don't worry, ma'am. Nobody's ever gotten seriously hurt on this slope. It's a baby hill. And most
people don't break their legs anyway. They break
their thumbs."

"Thumbs? How—?"

"With the ski pole when they fall. It's hard to
make newbies understand they have to let go and just
fall freely. They want to hang onto something and all
they've got is the pole. It whips around and *snap!*"

"Oh, that's a big comfort to know. Thanks."

The instructor grinned dazzlingly. "Don't worry,
I'll take good care of them. They're not as fragile as
mothers think."

*No, not physically, but you could break their hearts
with that smile,* Jane thought.

She sat watching them for a few more minutes and
decided their chances of ever getting to the top of the
hill were so remote that she didn't need to worry
about how they got back down. Each of them had already fallen a couple of times just trying to master
the awkward toes-out method of climbing. Right now
they were both lying facedown in the snow, laughing
uncontrollably.

Above them, Jane caught a glimpse of crimson and

noticed that it belonged, once again, to the skier she'd seen twice yesterday. He or she must be somebody who regularly did some kind of cross-country skiing. Maybe a local person. He—there was, Jane decided, something essentially masculine in the stride—stopped as she watched. Put binoculars—no, a camera—to his face. And then fumbled around in his jacket. It looked as if he'd taken out a small pad or book and might be writing something in it. How strange. Some kind of nature study or bird watching, no doubt.

As she glanced one last time at the girls, now trying to help each other up in a Keystone Kops manner, she noticed something new at the bunny slope. Over at the edge, near the woods that bordered the area, there was a snowman. Looking at it, she realized it was the first snowman she'd seen since being in the mountains. Apparently when people were surrounded by this much snow, they didn't think to use it for the usual games. This, however, was an elaborate one— short and squat, but quite big, with a tablecloth or something around its shoulders as a cape and something gold and sparkly on its head like a crown. It had sticks for arms and big mittens on the ends of the sticks.

Her timing was perfect. Shelley was just arriving at her cabin when she returned. "Let's go get breakfast. I'll tell you along the way."

"Mel must be going crazy," Shelley said when Jane had explained about Mel's problems with the sheriff after they'd found Doris.

"Uh-huh. He keeps claiming that he's on vacation and not interested, but he was pretty wild about the haphazard way the sheriff was treating the crime scene. If it *was* a crime scene. Mel's so meticulous, and this guy seems to be a lazy good ol' boy. A real conflict of styles of law enforcement, to say the least."

"What do you think?"

They were approaching the entrance to the hotel and slowed down. "I don't know," Jane said. "It seems real odd to me that the papers looked like they were thrown around after she died. Naturally, it could just happen that there weren't any where she fell, but it seems unlikely. You should have seen the place, Shelley. It looked like a tornado had gone through."

"Still . . ."

"I know. She had heart trouble and had a nasty afternoon. Before we go in where somebody might overhear us, let me tell you about my conversation last night with Lucky—"

When they went in to the restaurant, they made a point of getting an isolated table so they could continue to talk, albeit in near whispers.

"I'm with you on this, I think," Shelley said as they got settled. "She might well have died of natural causes, but when you factor in the mess in her place and that at least one person has a good reason to want her out of the way, you can't overlook the possibility of foul play."

"Tell me your impression of Stu Gortner," Jane said. "I didn't hear any of the debate and only met him for a minute. He winked at me."

"Ugh!"

The waiter appeared and invited them to either order from the menu or have the buffet breakfast. "I didn't think I'd ever hear myself say this, but I'm not very hungry," Jane said. "Could I just have some fruit and coffee?"

"We've got some nice papaya and kiwi," he began.

"No, just ordinary fruit. An apple, maybe?"

"No apples. But there are some peaches. How about one of those sliced over some cold cereal?" he suggested.

"Perfect. But plain cereal. Nothing with oats or nuts."

"Rice Krispies?"

"You're a good man."

"Make it two," Shelley put in.

When he'd brought their coffee, Shelley said, "Stu Gortner is a slick number. Utterly charming. Good-looking in an almost elder-statesman way, as you know. And he never really did one single thing to Mrs. Schmidtheiser that you could point to or repeat and say, 'That was rude.' It was much more subtle. It was the cumulative effect. He didn't quite interrupt her; he didn't quite make faces when she was talking; he didn't quite laugh when he repeated her points. But he danced real, real close."

"I guess from the way Mrs. Schmidtheiser tore out of the room that she was well aware that he was doing better than she was."

"I don't think she did realize that until near the end of the thing. At first she just kept bombing along, so absorbed in her own notes and documents and slides that she really didn't pay much attention to him. She'd talk; then, when he talked, she'd frantically rustle things around, getting ready for the next part of her presentation. But, toward the end, she seemed to catch on."

"In what way?"

"She started listening to him. He'd say something suave and amusing that cut her off at the knees and she'd gape and go all red in the face. I'd sure like to know what somebody like Lucky thought of it. After all, I don't know a thing about the 'content' of what they were saying."

"When he talked to me last night, he indicated that Gortner really didn't have anything to say on his own behalf—that he was only making Mrs. Schmidt-heiser's evidence look silly."

"Well, it did look that way to me, too, but there was a lot of talk about baptismal documents, FHC film numbers, something called *tafels*—God knows what that means I think it's some kind of list of all your relatives— Oh, here's Mel."

Jane waved and he joined them, looking grim.

"I got curious," he said abruptly as he sat down. "Called the sheriff. Seems they found an empty pill bottle in her purse. The residue in the bottle matched the residue in the coffee cup. Except the dosage in the cup was about twenty times what a person can take."

"You were right. It was murder," Jane said.

"I'm not the one who thought that, Jane," he reminded her. "And the sheriff told me that proved his theory. Suicide."

"Suicide?" Shelley exclaimed.

"Right," Mel said wryly. "She'd been humiliated in public over her research, so she came home, poured all her remaining heart-medicine pills into a cup of coffee, knocked it back, threw the offending research all over the room, and dropped dead in the one place where none of the papers had landed."

"What a dolt!" Jane said.

"Aren't you going to ask me what he said about fingerprints on the medicine bottle?" Mel flipped open the menu angrily.

"Okay. I'll bite," Jane said. "What was his response?"

"Silence! He obviously hadn't even thought about it. Probably every lab tech in the county handled the damned thing. Now, of course, he *has* to stick with this suicide thing or his job will go up in flames."

Jane considered this for a minute or two while Mel tried to calm down enough to read the menu. When he looked up, she said, "I think we ought to make damned sure that's exactly what happens."

"But I'm on vacation!" Mel said brokenly.

"And I hope you're enjoying it."

They all looked up guiltily. Tenny Garner had approached the table without any of them noticing.

"I—ah, yes. It's a great place you've got here," Mel said. "Will you join us?"

Tenny glanced around the room and said, "Maybe for a minute. I'm looking for Uncle Bill. You haven't seen him around, have you? He's disappeared."

10

Tenny took the chair next to Shelley's.

"When did somebody see him last?" Mel asked.

"Last night. After that poor woman died. I went to tell him and found him cleaning up the lost-and-found room."

"But what about your aunt?" Jane asked. "Didn't she see him after that?"

"No, he never came back to their place."

"Oh, dear—" Shelley said.

Tenny smiled. "No, no, don't worry. I didn't mean to alarm you. I'm certain he's just gone off to do a little hunting. He'll turn up in his own good time."

"Does he do that? Just go away without telling anyone?" Mel asked.

Tenny nodded. "Every once in a while. He's an old mountain man with only a thin veneer of civilization. Something nicks the veneer deep enough and he takes off. He'll turn up by lunchtime, muddy and bloody and as cheerful as a chipmunk. Well, maybe that's going too far. As cheerful as he's capable of being, I should say."

"Tenny, what did he really think about Mrs. Schmidtheiser's claim that he was the rightful Tsar?" Shelley asked.

Tenny thought for a minute. "That's really two

questions and I know the answer to only one of them. The first question is: is he the person she claims he is? And the second question is: does he want to act on it in any way? On the first, I have no idea. On the second, no way! He's not interested in politics. I don't believe he's ever even voted once in his life. Joanna is always telling him it's his patriotic duty, and he says anybody who wanted to try to run a country or even a county was crazy to begin with, so there was no difference between them."

"He could have a point," Jane said. "But hasn't he ever talked about who he is? Or rather, who his father was? Father or grandfather? I've forgotten already."

"His father," Tenny confirmed. "Oh, he talked about him some, but only to Aunt Joanna and me. And then not often. Mainly just things old Gregory had told him about hunting or mountain lore or nature."

"So you don't know anything about Gregory?" Mel asked.

"Oh, I know some. But most of it's from a local history book somebody here in the county did about twenty years ago. The author of the book was taken with the legend of old Gregory Smith and interviewed a lot of the old-timers about him. How accurate any of it was is anybody's guess."

She thought for a moment. "Old Gregory turned up in Colorado sometime in the 1920s, I believe. Nobody knew where he lived or what he did. He'd just show up from time to time and trade gold for supplies. Apparently he had a small mine someplace in the mountains. Or maybe a stream he was panning. Then, in about 1925 or so, he came out of the mountains with a substantial amount of gold, bought this land, married a local girl, and settled in. People figured his mine had played out, and he didn't exactly deny it, but he told folks he thought a man didn't have the right to take more from the earth than he needed."

"Interesting attitude," Mel said. "Sort of suggests there might be a mine still worth mining."

The waiter came with Jane's and Shelley's breakfasts, and Tenny's recital was halted while Mel ordered.

"One of the things Doris found out," Tenny went on when the waiter had gone, "was that the gold he used to buy the land was melted down into little ingots—I think that's what you call them."

"So?" Jane said.

"So it wasn't proper nuggets or dust out of the ground or a streambed. Doris thought it was melted-down jewelry rather than anything he mined."

"Could that be true?" Shelley asked.

Tenny shrugged. "I don't know much about it, but I don't think the process for melting down either nuggets or jewelry is awfully high-tech. Anyway, he married and the two children—my uncle Bill and his sister, Carol, who was Pete's mom—were born and then their mother died. Uncle Bill says he has no memory of her at all. Old Gregory stuck around after that. Did some hunting, a little farming, and some of the women from the tribe helped him raise his children. That's why Uncle Bill's always been so close to the tribe. Gregory died at just about the end of World War Two, when Bill was only sixteen, and Bill, who'd been hunting practically since he could walk, built the little hunters' cabins. There were about a dozen of them and a big cookhouse-lodge. A few of the cabins are still around. We use them for storage."

"What was Gregory like? What did he look like?" Jane asked.

Tenny shrugged again. "I never saw him. And as far as I know, nobody dared take a picture of him. He was known for not allowing it. Uncle Bill once said he had a picture of himself with his mother and father, but when I asked to see it, he hemmed and hawed and said he'd lost it. Years later, I asked him about it again and he said I'd imagined the conversation. So I don't know if there really is one or not. But even if there wasn't, don't assume that means anything. Most of the old-timers around here were like that. Private to the point of paranoia. The local history book has a drawing of Gregory, based on what people said he looked like. To tell the truth, the drawing resembles Rasputin more than it does any tsar," she said with a laugh. "Long, straggly beard, spooky-looking eyes. But then, half the men in the mountains used to look like that. Apparently a beard is real warm in the winter."

Jane noticed that Mel was gazing into the middle distance and stroking his chin. "Don't even think about it," she said.

He grinned. "You don't see me as a mountain man?"

"Was there anything else about him in the book that encouraged Doris in her claims?" Jane asked Tenny.

"Yes. The book said he spoke with a heavy, mysterious accent. And Uncle Bill did say that though his father couldn't read or write English, he kept his account books in something that looked like Russian."

"Looked like Russian? Couldn't that be determined pretty easily?" Jane asked.

"Yes, except that Gregory had Bill burn all of them when he—Gregory, that is—was sick with his final illness. At least that's what Uncle Bill said happened."

"You don't believe him?"

"I don't know. Uncle Bill's a very private man. He might have said that just so nobody would bug him about seeing the account books. Then again, he didn't need to even admit that he thought the writing was Russian, so it might well be true. There's also a highly questionable story the local historian picked up, about some Russian visitors here once who talked to Gregory in their native language and he was able to talk with them. I don't know that I buy that. There's never been a time I know of that Russian tourists happened through this area. I don't think you often find Russian tourists anywhere."

"Did you ever ask your uncle straight-out whether he thought his father was the person Doris Schmidtheiser claimed?" Jane asked.

"Oh, sure. About five years ago, when Doris found him and the group started meeting here. You know, that was Pete's doing. He loves all this silly stuff about Uncle Bill being the Tsar."

"He must be upset about Mrs. Schmidtheiser's death," Mel said.

"Frantic," Tenny agreed. "Since Uncle Bill and Aunt Joanna have no children, I think Pete has always seen himself as the 'heir presumptive.' Poor dolt."

"You mean he took it seriously?" Jane asked.

"Oh, he pretended to scoff, but he was always quietly getting together with Doris and her adherents. And trying to convince Uncle Bill to go along with it all. It's the sort of thing designed to appeal to him. Pete's not exactly into the work ethic. He works harder at trying to find an easy way to get rich than most people actually work at their jobs. He was a stockbroker in California before his mother died and he came here. I think he sailed pretty damned close to the wind and something went badly wrong. When he first came here, he asked us to tell anybody who called looking for him that we hadn't seen him for years. But whatever it was apparently blew over after a while."

"You don't like him much," Mel observed.

"Oh, he's really okay most of the time. Sort of an amiable fool. A rah-rah guy who's perfect for his job here. He'd have made a good entertainment director on a cruise ship. He's dumb and chirpy, except for an occasional burst of bad temper. Our customers here are on vacation. They don't want deep thoughts. And he buzzes around like a mindless goodwill ambassador. He's valuable in his own way, I guess. If he'd just stay in his proper place," she added grimly.

Mel picked up on her tone. "What do you mean?"

Tenny looked disconcerted. "I've blabbed too much already. I shouldn't be boring you with all this. It's not your problem."

"But it might soon be," Shelley said significantly.

Tenny stared at her for a long moment, then said, "Well, Uncle Bill gave orders that we were to be absolutely honest with the investors. I guess you might as well know. It doesn't matter anyway, except that it makes me mad."

"What's happened?" Shelley prodded.

"Pete had dinner with HawkHunter last night," Tenny said. "My spies tell me that he was giving HawkHunter a load of nonsense about how if he, Pete, were in charge of the sale of the resort, he'd make sure the tribe's rights to the top of the mountain would be respected."

Jane remembered seeing Pete and HawkHunter together in the Cigar Room. And she also remembered the waiter who had found so many little chores to do near their table.

"He also hinted to HawkHunter that Uncle Bill was so anxious to retire and get away that he might give Pete power of attorney to negotiate the sale of the resort on his behalf."

"Is that likely?" Shelley asked, alarmed.

"About as likely as our little mountain suddenly growing a peak!" Tenny said furiously. "God, no. Uncle Bill wouldn't trust Pete to buy a quart of milk and come back with the right change. I told you, it was just annoying and of no significance."

"There's more to this," Jane said.

"What are you, a mind reader?" Tenny asked with a strained laugh. "Yes, there's more. That idiot Pete had the nerve to suggest to HawkHunter that Uncle Bill was going a little batty and this mythical power of attorney might not be given entirely freely. The nice person in me keeps saying not to tattle to Uncle Bill about it, but the nasty little kid inside would like to pull up a lawn chair to the sidelines and watch the fireworks."

"Is that why you're looking for him?" Mel asked.

"No. I'm doing Aunt Joanna's bidding. She wants him reminded that he has a doctor's appointment this afternoon for the ingrown toenail he's been complaining about. She thinks he's gone missing on purpose so he can pretend he forgot about it. It takes an act of Congress to get him to a doctor."

"Forgive me for saying so, but he can't have been an easy husband for her to be married to all these years," Jane said. She'd finished her cereal and was wishing she'd gotten some bacon and toast with it. She was hungrier now than when she had started eating.

Tenny cheered up. "He'd be hell on wheels for most of us, but she adores him. They've never had children except for me in a way, and she's been mother and wife to him. Bossing him around, talking his ears off, surrounding him with ghastly little domestic stuff. They're perfect for each other."

"She told us you said she had no taste," Jane said with a smile.

Tenny laughed. "I never *said* that in my life."

"Don't worry. I saw the thing she's crocheting. And she seemed to take real pride in your taste."

"Excuse me, but we got sidetracked," Mel said. The waiter was back with his breakfast, a substantial order that Jane looked over longingly. "You want the muffin?" Mel asked.

She nearly snatched it. "Yes, thanks."

"You said you asked your uncle what he thought of Mrs. Schmidtheiser's claims," Mel said to Tenny. "What was his response?"

"Pretty much that she might be right and he didn't care. He said Gregory sometimes mentioned the Old Country in a vague way. He'd say the winters here weren't any worse than in the Old Country, that sort of remark."

"Could that mean Russia?" Jane asked.

"Sure. Or it could mean a mountainous area of Germany or Switzerland, or any part of Finland, for that matter," Tenny said.

"So he didn't care about the truth of it?"

"I don't think it was so much that he didn't care as it was that he understood and respected his father's privacy. If the old man didn't want anybody to know his background, then nobody—not even Bill himself—had any business snooping into it. He wasn't so fanatic about it that he really minded Doris and her pals, but he wasn't about to help them. It's a shame Doris couldn't have lived a few more years—"

She glanced around at their confused expressions. "I forget that you haven't been subjected to as much genealogy as we have. I meant the census. The government grants you privacy when you answer the census questions. For your lifetime. And it considers the average lifetime to be seventy years. So right now the most recent census that's available to the public is the one of 1920. Gregory could have been anywhere then. Maybe already up in the mountains someplace where no census taker could find him. Or maybe in transit from wherever he came from. But by 1930, he was right here, so in the year 2000 the genealogists can go to the National Archives and see his answers to the questions."

"What sort of questions?" Jane asked.

"I don't know what they asked in 1930, but in the previous ones they asked things like where and when you were born, where each of your parents was born, when you came to this country if you weren't born here, whether and when you took your citizenship. Things like that."

"So in 2000 they can find out more about him,"

Jane mused. "But would he have answered the questions the census people asked him? Or told the truth if he did?"

"Good point," Tenny said.

"The class I took yesterday talked about the census a little bit," Shelley put in. "The teacher said it wasn't always very reliable. Apparently they hired somebody—practically anybody who was available—to go around and ask the questions. If the census taker got sick of it, or drunk, or was a little hard of hearing, the answers might be pretty erroneous, even if they were given truthfully. And a lot of people always got missed. If they weren't home to answer that day, the census taker would often just ask the next-door neighbor."

"Oh, my God," Tenny said, glancing at her watch. "I've got a ton of things to do. Sorry for horning in on your breakfast. If you see Uncle Bill before I do, would you tell him I'm looking for him?"

Mel watched her leave. "I don't like it," he said softly.

"What don't you like?" Jane asked.

"Anybody who goes missing right after hearing about a mysterious death."

11

"So you've never skied before, either," Jane said.

They were bundled up and on their way to the bunny slope to take a ski lesson.

Shelley shook her head. "No, and I don't know why I let you talk me into it this time. A couple of grown women getting ready to tie sticks to their feet and slide down a hill! We've gone mad."

"Come on, Shelley. We're nineties-type women. We can do anything."

"That's what you said about that step-aerobics class, and you didn't last through one session."

"Well, it was stupid and boring."

"And hard! And remember the 'Drawing on the Right Side of Your Brain' class you talked me into going to with you?"

"That teacher should have been fired. Imagine telling us we didn't *have* right sides to our brains," Jane said with a grin. "We must. Otherwise our heads would be lopsided."

"I think this is going to be worse," Shelley predicted. "I can see this going right off the top of the humiliation scale."

"But, Shelley, everybody skis. Celebrities ski. We might run into Cher or some Kennedys or Bob Denver—"

"I think you mean John Denver. And I don't imagine you'll be brushing elbows with any of them on the bunny slope of this resort. Why isn't Mel coming along to help us?"

"He's still crippled from yesterday. Besides, he's asking around about Bill. It's really galling him being an outsider with no authority, especially since the sheriff is such a casual good ol' boy. I keep telling him to look at it as a valuable learning experience, and he just growls."

"You ladies here for a little practice?" a handsome young man asked.

"No, lessons. We've never skied before," Jane replied.

"Then you've come to exactly the right place," he said. "I'm an instructor and I'm just putting a little class together. Sit down right here while I fit some other folks with their boots and skis, and I'll be back to you in a minute."

"You don't think somebody ought to be worried about Bill disappearing?" Shelley asked as they sat down on a bench next to the little equipment shop.

"Tenny doesn't seem too worried. More irritated than concerned, I'd say. And she certainly knows him best. I can't imagine anybody simply taking off like that in the midst of trying to sell this place, but he's clearly a pretty strange individual. Say, I've been wondering about something that's probably none of my business. . . ."

"Don't let that stop you from asking," Shelley said, smiling.

"Well, if Paul and his group of investors buy this place, will that put Tenny out of work?"

"Good Lord, no! Paul says it looks like the place

is run wonderfully. It really comes down to purely financial considerations: taxes, interest rates on various financing options, consolidation of some old improvement loans. Boring stuff like that. Dreadful Pete wouldn't even be out of a job."

"Okay, Bunnies, are you ready?"

The handsome young man was back.

"Let's get you fitted out and ready to turn into Olympic material!"

"Does he have to be so damned perky?" Shelley said under her breath.

"Shelley, we need all the help we can get, and if Perky Power will do any good, I'm all for it."

The instructor, who claimed his name was Gavin ("A likely story!" Shelley huffed), asked them their height, weight, and experience. They gave their height, lied about their weight, and admitted to no experience whatsoever. "In skiing, that is," Jane added. "I'm a world-class roller skater."

He stared at her.

"It was a joke," she said. "I don't think humor is his strong suit," she whispered to Shelley.

"Nor yours," Shelley whispered back.

Pseudo-Gavin got them fitted with ski boots and skis as well as poles the sizes of which were based on their height and fictional weight. Then he half dragged, half shoved them into line with four other beginners, two men and two women, all of whom looked faintly familiar. Jane suspected they were escapees from the genealogy convention.

"Listen up, Bunnies," Gavin said. "I want to explain your equipment to you. First, your poles. Put your wrist through the thong. That way, if you let go by accident, the pole won't go flying off and hit somebody else or get lost in the snow. Second, don't hook your thumb through the thong. Very important."

Jane shuddered, remembering the other instructor yesterday talking about broken thumbs.

"Since you're all beginners, I've set the latches on your boots to release the skis very easily. As you get better, we'll tighten that up. If you need to unlatch them, press your pole onto this latch at the back of your heel." He demonstrated.

"Now, to skiing, Bunnies!" he continued. "The first thing you need to learn is how to fall down."

One of the men said, "That's the one thing I'm afraid I know how to do! Har, har!"

Gavin's expression was the strained smile of a man who had heard this hilarious line too many times to count. "With respect, sir, you probably don't."

Then, to the whole group: "Until you learn a bit about skiing, you'll probably go out of control a couple times and at first you won't be able to regain control, so you need to know how to stop. The first way to stop, if you're not going very fast and are just a little wobbly, is to toe-in." He demonstrated. "This looks like it will just run your skis across each other, so you also want to ankle-in so you're digging into the surface. Remember that: toe-in, ankle-in."

They all nodded and tried to ankle-in wearing boots that felt like they were made from discarded iron frying pans.

"Now, I'm going to go up the hill just a little ways and demonstrate. And while I'm doing that, I'm going to show you the two ways of going uphill. You're in position for the first way." They were all standing in a line with their skis parallel to the slope. "You just step sideways. Try a step or two."

Gingerly, Jane took a tiny step up the hill with her right foot, then followed with her left. Ah, not so hard, she was thinking. She was ready to try another step when the man at the front of their little line started to lose his balance. He leaned forward. Pitched backward. Forward again. And backward as if he'd been pushed. He crashed into Shelley, who crashed into Jane, who crashed into the woman behind her. Amid shrieks and startled yelps, they all went down like a row of dominoes. Skis and poles flew everywhere.

"We look like a bus accident in the Alps," Jane said, laughing and spitting out a mouthful of snow. The rest of the accident victims thought it was very jolly, too.

Gavin, on the other hand, stood looking to heaven as if pleading with God to take them all now and put him out of his misery.

"Anybody hurt?" he finally asked grimly. He sounded as if he sincerely hoped so.

Giggling like children and making inane jokes about snow being soft, they managed to get back on their feet. After some delay, all the poles and skis were sorted out and put back on. Gavin, his professionally perky demeanor restored, went back to his lecture. "Maybe I should have told you first about the other way of falling down. It would have saved us this mess. If you're completely out of control or fear you're going to be, just sit down. Don't lean forward. Don't try to get your balance back. Don't reach for anything or try to use your poles. Just SIT DOWN!"

"What do you suppose Gavin is in the summer?" Jane asked under her breath.

"A Trappist monk, if he's smart," Shelley hissed

back. "After working with dummies like us for three quarters of the year, he probably needs the quiet."

"This from a woman who's head of the Room Mother Committee three-quarters of the year."

"I'm thinking about applying what I'm learning here to that job. The 'when in doubt, just sit down' part might play, but I wouldn't dare give them pointed poles."

Jane laughed so hard she nearly lost her balance again and had to practice the fast-sit technique.

Gavin finally demonstrated stairstepping up the slope and then coming to a gentle stop on the way down by toeing-in ankling-in. Then he went back up, showing them how to walk in a sort of herringbone pattern with their toes pointing out.

"Can you hear that sound?" Shelley asked, watching him.

"What sound?"

"That screaming noise. It's my thighs, just thinking about trying to do that!"

"Never mind. We'll just stairstep it."

Gavin then made a spectacular show of pretending to lose his balance and sitting down in place. It all looked graceful, fun, and easy when he did it. He got up and glided effortlessly to a spot about ten feet uphill from them. "Okay, Bunnies, come up where I am and we'll take our first downhill run."

They obediently stairstepped their way up to him, and he picked Shelley to go first. He got next to her, whispered a bit of encouragement, showed her how to get her skis turned around and pointing the right way without her tripping, and she was off. She was moving so slowly it was almost imperceptible, but she picked up a little speed as she went along. She was going at a slow-walk pace by the time she got to the flat area below. Gavin, right next to her the whole way, said, "Toe-in, ankle-in now!"

Shelley did so, came to a stop, and grinned at Jane over her shoulder. "I'm a skier now!" she yelled. "Can I quit?"

"No way! We're doing this whole hill before you get to quit," Jane shouted back.

Jane was next and did a decent job, though it couldn't have looked as steady and well balanced as Shelley's performance. When she got stopped, she realized she'd been holding her breath the whole time. "Wow! It's sort of like riding down an escalator that's going too fast!" she said.

The next person to try it was a rather heavy woman in a daffodil-colored ski outfit. Having watched Shelley's and Jane's sedate descents, she decided to put a little oomph into it. She actually shoved off with her poles instead of letting gravity seduce her along. This was a nasty surprise to Gavin, and he was yelling at her to toe-in, ankle-in before she got three feet forward. She either couldn't manage or didn't want to, and shot between Jane and Shelley, across the flat area, past the equipment hut, and well out in the parking lot, her skis scraping horribly on exposed bits of asphalt, before she remembered the sitting-down technique.

The other three managed well enough and Gavin took them all back up the hill again. A little farther this time. After their second mini-runs, Gavin proclaimed Jane, Shelley, and a wiry older man sufficiently skilled to go off and practice on their own.

"Okay, here's the deal," Shelley pronounced. "We're going clear to the top of the hill. Then we're coming back down by whatever method works out best and no matter how many times we fall along the way. Then we're retiring. Just think, for the rest of our lives we can say We Have Skied. And nobody will ever be able to say, 'But you must try it once.' So we'll never have to do it again."

"Sounds like a good plan to me. Is there food at the end of this scenario? You didn't mention food."

"There's a huge lunch, Jane."

"Okay."

They started laboriously stairstepping their way up the hill. After about ten minutes, during which she had to look at her feet to make sure they were doing the right thing, Jane stopped. "Jeez! We should be clear to the top by now. And we're still at the bottom."

"Keep going, Jane," Shelley said. "Think about lunch."

"There's that person again," Jane said, shading her eyes and looking up at the top of the hill.

"Which person?"

"I don't know. Just a person I keep seeing. He has cameras and binoculars. A nature nut, I imagine."

"Jane, stop talking."

They stairstepped some more, and it was Shelley this time who wanted to stop. "Look at that! We're nearly halfway up the hill."

"We could just go from here."

"No, we're going to the top. Once. Look at the cute snowman."

"Hadn't you noticed him before? He appeared overnight."

"What's he got on his head?"

"I think it's supposed to be a crown."

"I know, but what is it really?"

"I dunno. Maybe one of those sort of fluted fruit bowls? Remember the gold plastic ones we used for that PTA fund-raising party with a Tropical Holiday theme? To quote a friend of mine, stop talking!"

After two more rest stops, they reached the top of the hill and sat down to get their breath. "Wow! This is neat up here," Jane gasped. "Look, the whole resort's laid out like a map. You should have brought a camera along. You could have taken a picture for Paul so when he gets home and wonders just where the various buildings and wings are, you'd have it. Are you ready to go?"

"Not yet. I'm never coming here again for the rest of my life, so I want to appreciate it for a few minutes. The snowman looks weird from the back. Just the cape and crown showing."

Jane was gazing around behind them. "The Indians who were demonstrating said there was a graveyard up here. It doesn't look like that to me."

"Jane, it's covered with snow. How would you know? You expect to see a mausoleum or a totem pole or something sticking up?"

"Hmmm. You have a point. It's certainly flat enough to make a good cemetery. Looks like somebody took a gigantic knife to it and sliced the top off. You could land a 747 along here."

Shelley was hoisting herself to her feet. "Speaking of landing, are we ready to take off?"

"I guess so. It sure looks a lot steeper from the top."

"How are we going to do this? One at a time all the way down?"

"Okay. Who goes first?"

"I do. I want to get this over with."

Shelley took a deep breath, turned her skis forward, and started gently drifting away. She picked up speed gradually until, apparently feeling it was too much of a good thing, she sat down suddenly, plowing a bit of a trench before she came to a complete stop. She yelled up to Jane, "Come this far and we'll go the rest of the way together."

Jane set out, cleverly charting a course a little farther left than Shelley had gone so that she wouldn't run over her. The first few minutes were okay. She started going a little faster, discovered that she could actually breathe at the same time she skied. And a little faster yet. She tried toeing-in to slow herself, but that just made her veer more to the left. Maybe, she thought frantically, it was toe-out. She glanced down at her feet, which was how she made her fatal mistake. When she looked back up a second later, she realized she was headed toward the woods. Specifically, straight for the snowman just on the edge of the woods.

She tried to sit down, but was leaning too far forward. *Crouch!* she told herself frantically, but she was so tense that her knees just wouldn't get the message.

With a terrific mental effort, she made her legs go limp and sat down. By that time she was moving so fast that she kept going for another five feet, sending up a spray of snow. The thing that finally stopped her was the snowman. She didn't so much crash into it, for her speed had diminished considerably, as bump into it firmly. Very firmly.

The snowman's head rolled off, sending the crown/bowl spinning across the snow.

"Jane! Are you all right?" Shelley yelled from someplace off to her right.

"I'm okay," Jane said, trying to stand up. Where had her skis gone? she was wondering. If they'd buried themselves in the snow, how would she ever find them? Still shaky from her adventure, she leaned on the snowman, placing her gloved hand where its head had been. But as she did so, the whole front section of the snow crumbled away in a slab.

And there, inside the snowman where there should have been nothing but more snow, was the body of Bill Smith.

— 12 —

It was another hour before Jane and Shelley could get away. The sheriff and his deputy had been summoned, people had been questioned extensively (especially Jane, who had discovered the body), the bunny slope had been cleared of skiers, and finally the earthly remains of Bill Smith had been taken away. By that time Jane and Shelley were frozen clear through. They hadn't been allowed to do anything but sit impatiently on the bench next to the equipment hut.

"At the risk of seeming insensitive, I'm starving," Shelley admitted when they were finally allowed to leave.

"Me, too," Jane said. "Let's go get some sandwiches at the lodge and take them to one of our cabins. I wish I knew where Mel was. He should have been there before the sheriff and his crew of bumblers trampled everything. I guess that's not really fair to say. They seemed to be taking it very seriously this time."

"I wonder if the sheriff is going to look more closely into Mrs. Schmidtheiser's death now."

"Surely he'll have to," Jane said. "I didn't like the way he started asking me more questions when he realized I was the one who had found her, too."

118

"It's just a weird coincidence, Jane."

"You and I know that, but that's when he asked me how I knew them both before I came here. Not *if* I knew them, but *how* I knew them. Shelley, I'm really uneasy about this."

The atmosphere at the lodge was subdued. Apparently word that the proprietor of the hotel had died had filtered down through the guests. And though few of them had ever seen him, much less met him, the news clearly dampened everyone's spirits. There was no sign, of course, of Tenny, Joanna, or Pete.

"Jane, you order us some sandwiches and chips and maybe some salad," Shelley said. "I'm going to give Paul a quick call on the house phone and see where all the kids are and what they're up to. I don't like not knowing exactly where they are."

"Me, neither. Keep an eye out for Mel, too, would you?"

Jane ordered plenty of sandwiches, assuming that they might end up feeding children as well as themselves. Even if the sandwiches weren't consumed right away, they'd have them for snacking. Shelley came back as Jane was settling in front of the fireplace in the main lounge. "Got the food yet?"

Jane shook her head. "They're real busy. It'll take about ten more minutes."

"Okay. I've got everybody accounted for. Katie and Denise have taken the shuttle to town to shop at the music store. Mike is skiing with the girl he met yesterday," she said, ticking them off on her fingers as she spoke. "Todd and John are playing Nintendo in Mel's cabin and they want lunch."

"I ordered lots of extra sandwiches. Did you find Mel?"

"Yes, and he's meeting us at your cabin."

"Did he know about Bill?"

"Yes. Don't sidetrack me. I'll forget the rest of my list. Paul's leaving in an hour. He says that naturally their negotiations have been put on hold and he thinks it would be bad for the investors to hang around looking like vultures waiting to pounce on the grieving widow."

"Oh, dear. I guess we should all go, shouldn't we?"

"No, no reason to. In fact, he asked me to stay on to attend the funeral. And it would cost the absolute earth to get plane tickets on such short notice for all of us. If you don't mind, I'll just move in with you, though."

"Fine by me."

Ever efficient, Shelley nodded and continued. "Now, if you'll wait for the sandwiches and bring them along, I'll go ahead, say good-bye to Paul, grab my stuff, then get a nice fire started in your cabin so we can get good and warm. I'm not sure I'm capable of getting warm again, but I'd like to give it a shot. Let me have your key."

And without any more fuss, she was gone. Jane marveled, as she had so often over the years of their friendship, at how well organized Shelley was under the slightest pressure. She seemed to be able to pluck information out of the air—her rapid determination of where all the children had gone was proof of that—and to make quick, sensible decisions whenever they were required.

Jane waited another ten minutes and went back to the carryout section of the restaurant. Linda Moosefoot was waiting there, too. Her eyes were red.

"Oh, Mrs. Jeffry, I was just on my way to your cabin. Do you mind if I have a fast lunch first? I should have been there an hour ago, but what with . . ." Her voice trailed off and she sniffed.

"Good heavens! Don't think about it. There's no need to tidy up after us."

"No, I'm glad to have something to do."

"Then bring your lunch along and eat it with us. I'm waiting for sandwiches."

Just as she spoke, the waiter came through the door from the kitchen, took a look at her, and slapped his forehead. "Shit," he muttered and then looked even more upset that she'd heard him.

"You lost my order?" Jane asked.

"I'm so sorry. We had a cancellation of an order and I think I canceled yours by mistake."

"No harm done. Let's start over."

Linda said, "Give him your order and I'll bring it along with mine."

"Thanks. My toes are numb. I have to get these boots off to see if they're still alive," Jane said.

As she reached her cabin, actively shivering now, Shelley opened the door. "I've dumped my stuff in the bedroom and the fire is going. Come in. You look half dead yourself."

They didn't talk about the body until Jane had replaced her boots with warm, fuzzy slippers and was huddled in front of the fireplace.

Shelley had fixed them both hot cocoa. "I thought it was better for shock," she said, handing Jane a steaming mug.

Mel arrived a minute later. He was both angry and concerned. "I should have known, if there was a murder victim anywhere within a ten-mile radius, that you'd stumble onto it," he said to Jane.

"Not so much a stumble as a slide," she said, her voice weak.

"Are you all right?" he asked contritely.

"Fine. Just cold and hungry."

"Tell me what happened."

Jane recounted her collision with the snowman. "That's why it was so large and squat. Bill Smith's body was inside the body of it. He was in a sitting position. It looked like the snow had been piled up around him, and then I guess the snowball head was stuck on top of the pile. Putting aside the fact that murder is unthinkable in itself, why on earth would anybody do anything so bizarre?"

Mel said, "Not so bizarre, really. If you hadn't run into it, the chances are that nobody would have found him until summer."

"Ugh!" Shelley said. "Just imagine—"

"Better not to," Mel said. "By then the chances of anybody remembering when the snowman had appeared would be almost nil. All possible witnesses would have been long gone, and half would have forgotten most of the details of their stay here. And there certainly wouldn't be any question of physical evidence—time of death, footprints, anything like that."

"But footprints are really a lost cause," Jane said. "By the time the sheriff's people got there, the whole area was trampled. And anyway, it had snowed overnight and covered them up. I do remember when I was heading for the thing, there wasn't a mark anywhere near it. And I would imagine packing a body in snow would make havoc of body temperature. Not only is snow cold, but I understand it's an insulator. At least the gardening programs say so."

"Tell me what the sheriff's people did," Mel said.

"They actually seemed fairly thorough. They took a lot of photographs. They brought two toboggans up the hill. One for Bill, and the other to put the snow on as they removed it from around the body. They packed the snow into plastic containers and labeled them."

Mel nodded. "Good. They can melt it down and check for fabric fibers. What else?"

"Well, after they took the body away, they dug a big circle around where it had been. I mean dug the snow, not the ground. The woods must act as some kind of windbreak or snow fence. The snow wasn't awfully deep right there. They took away a lot of samples of that, too. I guess they were looking for anything the murderer might have dropped."

"Not necessarily the murderer, keep in mind," Mel said absently, gazing past her at the fire.

"What do you mean?" Shelley asked. She had gone to the kitchen and came back with a third mug of cocoa for Mel.

"Nothing, really. Just that the person who killed him and the person who put him in the snowman aren't necessarily the same. They probably are, but that's not proof."

"But why else would anybody build the snowman around him if they didn't kill him?" Jane asked.

"I don't know. A grisly prank, maybe? I didn't mean to suggest that it was likely, just that you can't afford to jump to any conclusions with something like this. Did the sheriff say it was murder? Smith didn't, by any chance, die of natural causes, did he?"

"No, the sheriff said there was clearly a violent blow to the head. Fortunately, I didn't see that much. I only saw his shirt and hand and knew it was a person; then I screamed and turned away. I didn't find him on purpose, you know," she added, harking back to his earlier criticism.

"I know. I'm sorry I was nasty about it. It's just that you do have a way of finding bodies."

"The sheriff mentioned that, too. Rather pointedly. It's a talent I do nothing to encourage," she said wryly.

He nodded and changed the subject. "Do you have anything to eat here?"

"Linda Moosefoot is bringing our lunch with hers. She should be along any minute now."

And as if summoned by the thought, Linda opened the door, calling out, "Hello? Mrs. Jeffry?"

"Come in, Linda."

Mel and Shelley extended their sympathies to her on the death of her employer.

"To tell the truth, he wasn't a really likable man," Linda said. "But I'm sorry he's dead. His ties to our tribe go back a long way. We have good reason to be grateful to him. They're saying it was murder. Is that true?"

"I think so," Mel replied. "Who's saying that?"

Linda shrugged. "Everybody. Well, finding him in a snowman . . . and all the sheriff's people . . . what else could people think?"

"True enough," Mel admitted.

"How are Tenny and Joanna doing?" Jane asked.

"Pretty well. They were expecting it, after all."

"What?" Mel exclaimed.

"Oh, I don't mean that he'd be murdered. Nobody

expected that. But that he'd die. See, he had a very bad heart condition. Not too many people knew. He was real private about his life. But he'd had a couple heart attacks, a pacemaker, angio-whatever. All of that. I guess that's why he was so anxious to sell the resort and retire in what little time he had left. Tenny asked those who knew about it to keep very quiet. They didn't want the investors to be swayed one way or the other by knowing. I guess they didn't want anyone to think they were desperate to sell—or to feel sorry for him. Either is likely. I s'pose I shouldn't be telling you now, but it doesn't matter anymore."

Shelley had prepared yet another cup of cocoa and handed it to Linda before starting to unpack the food from the insulated bags Linda had brought along.

"Thanks, Mrs. Nowack. Anyway, Tenny and Joanna had known for a long time that he could literally go at any minute, and I think in a way they'd already done some of their grieving, if that makes sense."

"Who knew about this?" Mel asked.

"Not too many people," Linda said. "A lot of the tribe, of course, knew he'd been in the hospital a couple times, but I don't think many of them realized how seriously ill he was. I knew only because Tenny's car broke down and I had to drive her down to Denver one time when he'd had one of his attacks. He'd collapsed in a store there and Tenny was really upset. His doctor knew, naturally. Pete Andrews must know, I assume. I don't know who else. Why does it matter?"

"I don't imagine it does," Mel said. "But I was

thinking that anybody who wanted him dead really only had to wait a while. Is that true?"

"I guess so."

"So maybe the people who *did* know about his condition would have less reason to take matters into their own hands. But it really wasn't common knowledge, it sounds like."

"No, I don't think so. The time I had to drive Tenny to Denver, everybody else was told he was in Florida, looking for property to buy to retire to. He was very secretive about his personal life. People up here in the mountains tend to be that way. Especially if it has to do with bad health or bad luck. They have a great horror of being pitied."

"Then it's doubly sad that he had to die—*and* be found as he was," Jane said quietly.

13

Jane and Shelley refused to let Linda clean for them when she'd finished her lunch. This was partly consideration, but partly a desire to talk over the implications of Bill Smith's murder with complete freedom from eavesdroppers. Linda left to do Mel's cabin and took the boys' lunches with her. Mel accompanied her, saying he needed to make some phone calls.

But before leaving, he took Jane aside for a moment. "What did you mean about the sheriff mentioning that you found the bodies? Both of them. He wasn't actually suspicious of you, was he?"

"I don't know. I think maybe so," she said, shivering.

"I'll sort this out," he said coldly.

"I think he's going to try to wring information out of the sheriff at the same time he tells him off and will come back mad as hell," Jane said to Shelley as she closed the door behind them.

"Maybe not. The sheriff might not mind his help now that he has a clear-cut murder on his hands. Tell him off about what?"

"Me. What's this?" Jane asked, picking up a book on the floor next to the sofa.

Shelley looked. "It must be Linda's. That backpack

thing of hers was open. It probably fell out. Oh, it's
a copy of *I, HawkHunter*. In paperback. I wonder if
they have it at the little bookstore here. It would be
interesting to read it again now that we've seen him
in person."

Shelley took the book and glanced at it, then
turned it over. "You'd think they'd have put a new
publicity picture on the back. This must have been
the original. What a nerdy-looking kid he was when
this was published. Imagine having a best-seller when
you're what—twenty-two or -three?"

Jane gazed at the picture. "Isn't it a shame that
men get so much better-looking as they get older and
we just fall apart?"

"Speak for yourself, girlie-girl," Shelley said in an
old-crone voice.

Jane took the book back and continued to stare at
the photo. "Shelley, this isn't just a matter of graceful
aging." She giggled. "Look at the nose. The man
doesn't have that nose this week."

"Good Lord! You're right. That's a little, ordinary
nose. And his hair has a bit of curl in the picture. You
could use it for a ruler now." She laughed. "The vanity of the man! I guess he thought he didn't look Indian enough."

"I'll catch Linda and give this back," Jane said,
jamming her feet into her boots, cozy now from having been in front of the fire. She took Willard along
for a romp.

When she returned, she said, "Well, Watson? What
do you think?"

"What do you mean 'Watson'? Don't I ever get to
be Holmes?"

Jane took off her boots and put them back in the

closet by the door. "I don't think you can get away from the fact that this must have something to do with the Tsar business—what with both Doris Schmidtheiser and Bill Smith dying."

"The Tsar is dead. Long live the Tsar," Shelley said.

"Pete? You think so?"

"It's certainly the obvious guess. Bill didn't want to have anything to do with it, but Tenny said Pete encouraged poor old Doris. Didn't she say he was the one who first hooked up with the Holnagrad Society and got them to have their annual meetings here? And if Bill was, by their estimation, the rightful Tsar and had no children of his own, Pete is the heir to the throne."

"But, Shelley—it's all so absurd! How could anybody take it seriously? The last Tsar died nearly eighty years ago. Why would anybody in their right mind think Russia wants another one?"

"Oh, I don't know. I actually heard a program on CNN a couple months ago and some political science professor was saying the only thing that could prevent a dozen civil wars in the former Russian entity was the restoration of a monarchy. For unification. More symbolic than real, I think he meant."

"I'll bet it's only him, three history buffs, and some psychic in Ohio who believe that," Jane scoffed.

"Well, there are different kinds of 'serious,' you know. Like that other guy—what's his name? Stu somebody? The guy Lucky was so upset with. He's got his own candidate for the position and he doesn't seem to make any pretense that he wants to put the guy on the nonexistent throne. He just wants to make a bunch of money off of him. There can be an awful lot of money in simply *being* a celebrity. Maybe Pete saw himself that way. The rightful heir. Movies. Maybe a book. Who knows?"

"But you heard what Linda Moosefoot said. Bill could have died at any minute anyway. Why not just wait?"

"You've got me."

Jane thought for a moment. "There might be some reason. I don't know—wait. Remember Lucky telling us that the last Tsar abdicated on his own behalf and that of his son—the little boy with the disease—"

"Hemophilia."

"Right. Well, suppose Bill was getting fed up with all the foolishness and had decided to sort of symbolically do the same thing. Abdicate on his own behalf and that of his heirs. He might do something like that just to get Doris and her people out of his hair. A man knowing he hadn't long to live and wanting to finish out his life in peace and quiet—? I don't mean it happened that way, only that it's possible there was some 'time pressure,' if you will. Some reason Pete couldn't just wait in line patiently."

Shelley shrugged. "I guess it's possible. Or maybe Bill knew his father wasn't the guy Doris thought he was and had finally decided it was time to tell her so. It all came down to what he knew, after all. His father might have told him about his childhood in Minneapolis or some place and Bill never saw any reason to mention it, thinking it was none of their business. From what Linda says, he'd have been like that. Not confirming or denying the story, because to do either would involve telling personal things he didn't want to share."

Jane nodded. "It would be in character for him, that's for sure. But if he knew that he wasn't what they thought, and knew he was going to die soon, he might have wanted to get Pete out of the whole business before he made a spectacle of himself and made Bill himself look silly after he was dead and gone and couldn't do anything about it."

Shelley frowned. "But how does either of those scenarios fit in with Doris?"

"Hmmm. Good point. If Pete wanted the 'title,' Doris would be his strongest supporter, you'd think. She's the one who had done all the research, gotten her followers convinced. He'd need her."

"Unless she didn't recognize him as Bill's heir to the title."

"Why wouldn't she? Unless Bill had a son nobody else knows about."

"Pretty thin, that," Shelley said.

"Well, suppose, then, that Bill had decided to abdicate for both of them, like we were speculating. Wouldn't Doris have to recognize such a gesture as valid?"

"Sure. Because it's the last Tsar's abdication that made Bill's right to the title valid in her eyes."

"And if Bill had already told her before he told Pete, Pete would have to get rid of her before she could lead her crowd off to find the next one in line."

"If it happened. I mean, if Bill had abdicated. And we have absolutely no reason on earth to think he had, except that it's a possibility."

"True, but the same applies to the other scenario. If Bill knew his father wasn't who they thought and had told Doris so, it would still put Pete out of the running and he'd have to shut her up before she could talk about it to anybody else."

"Okay, supposing either of those is true, when would Bill have told her? She stormed out of that debate and you found her dead a couple of hours later. He'd have had to tell her during that time. Why right then, after all these years?"

"Because of the debate," Jane said. "Was he there?"

"I have no idea. I was near the front of the room and wasn't exactly taking the roll. It was a pretty big crowd."

"Don't you see? He might have been a cold, remote man, but if he'd seen poor Doris being made a complete fool of on his behalf—even though he didn't want her to take up his cause—mightn't he have felt so sorry for her that he finally decided to put an end to it? Not let her go out and have that humiliation again?"

Shelley nodded. "That does make sense. And then he disappeared right after Tenny told him about Doris being found dead."

"Oh! Yes, he might have thought it was suicide, like the sheriff seemed determined to believe, and blame himself for taking away the thing she seemed to live for. Or he might have suspected Pete of having a hand in it and gone to have it out with him. Harsh words between them. Pete sees his whole future as a would-be Tsar and all the fame and fortune slipping away and he kills his uncle."

"Unfortunately, it's all in our imaginations. We haven't any reason whatsoever to believe that any of this happened. And even if it did, we could still be terribly wrong. I mean, what if Bill told Doris he wasn't Tsar or refused to be and she really did commit suicide? And then Bill himself was killed for some entirely different reason. His death and hers might not have anything to do with each other."

"I'd find it hard to believe. Too coincidental."

"But, Jane, coincidences *do* happen. All the time."

"That's true. I'll get that," Jane added as the phone rang. "Hello? Yes, she's right here. Front desk for you, Shelley."

Shelley took the phone. "Yes? He did? I'll come get them. Thanks."

She hung up and looked around for her boots. "Paul left his prescription sunglasses at the desk when he was checking out. I need to go get them before they get shuffled off to the lost-and-found. Want to come with me?"

"Sure. I'm out of cigarettes anyway and need to buy a pack."

"When are you going to really and truly quit?" Shelley asked with the superior tone of a woman who had quit smoking several years earlier.

"Someday. Maybe. Possibly very soon, when I find out what a pack costs from a machine at a resort."

As they went down the road—the solitude of the path through the woods wasn't at all appealing with a murderer around—Jane said, "I don't want the kids out of our sight again until we leave. Mel's with the little boys, but I want to know where Katie and Denise are."

"We'll hang out at the lodge watching for the shuttle. It drops people right at the door. We'll grab them as they get off. And Mike has to come back that way as well."

"It's *really* too expensive to go home now?"

"Jane, a last-minute ticket would probably cost six or seven hundred dollars. Each."

"No! Aren't there exceptions?"

"Sure, but running away from a murder scene, especially when you've found two of the bodies, isn't one of them."

"So nice of you to remind me," Jane said wryly. "Damn! That sheriff, Bumblefoot or whoever he is, would dearly love to pin this on me, I'll bet. I'm a nice, handy outsider."

"Don't worry. Nobody could seriously imagine that you had anything to do with either one. And Mel may know a whole lot more next time we talk to him."

"We *need* to know a whole lot more. Especially about Bill's death."

"In what way?"

"Where he died, for one thing," Jane said. "If he was killed someplace else, it obviously means it had to have been a strong man, or maybe even two people, who moved him to the side of the bunny slope. But if he was killed right there, it could have been anyone. All the killer had to do was prop him up where he fell and put the snow around him."

"True. And we're assuming it was Pete because he's the first one who occurred to us. Yet it could have been almost anyone."

"Yes, but the obvious person is usually the guilty one."

"But we don't know these people very well," Shelley pointed out. "And from what little we saw of Bill Smith, he wasn't exactly a bundle of charm. In fact, he was a downright unpleasant person. Who knows who else he might have offended?"

"But people don't kill somebody because they're offended. It takes a lot more than that. A real threat to their well-being, or a long hatred that finally comes to a head, or even raging greed."

"How do we know Bill wasn't surrounded by people with all of those motives, and maybe others as well? And it's entirely possible that his death had nothing to do with this whole silly Tsar thing. Maybe it had to do with selling the resort for that matter. There might be somebody local who's really upset about that. Somebody in the tribe. They're the ones who were demonstrating against him, after all."

A couple was approaching them from the other direction. They smiled and nodded as they passed, and were quiet until they were out of hearing range.

"But that demonstration was all so peaceful," Jane objected. "Almost downright friendly. And the protest was aimed as much at the potential investors as it was at Bill Smith. If they were murderous, would they have staged something so orderly and then done something so violent?"

"I don't mean the whole tribe, Jane. But one individual might really dislike him. He had a long history with them. And maybe somebody in the tribe or another neighbor thought he was about to sell the resort and move away for good, and it was their last chance to get at him."

Jane pondered this. "Murder is such an unthinkable way to solve problems that it's hard to imagine what could be in the mind of a person who would resort to it."

As they came to the front door of the lodge, a shuttle was arriving. They waited to see if any of their children got off it, and when they didn't, the women went inside. The lobby was strangely quiet. Tenny, of all people, was just coming out from behind the front desk.

"Tenny!" Jane exclaimed. "You're not working today. Surely—"

"Just came in to sort out a brawl," Tenny said angrily.

"A brawl?"

"Yes. Pete just had a fight with HawkHunter. Bloodied his nose and knocked some of his teeth out."

14

"Tenny, for heaven's sake, come sit down," Shelley said firmly as she took her elbow.

Tenny seemed to almost collapse against Shelley for a second, then got a grip on herself and straightened up. "Maybe I'd better. Thanks."

"Have you eaten anything this afternoon?" Jane asked as they led her toward the more casual of the two dining rooms.

"No, but I'm not—"

"You must eat something. Really. You'll feel much better," Jane insisted. She'd been waiting most of her life for somebody to say that to her. So far, nobody ever had.

The room was nearly empty. Even the latest lunchers had gone and the earliest dinner customers hadn't started arriving. The hostess seated them well away from the few other eaters after expressing condolences to Tenny, who received the remarks with preoccupied courtesy.

"Just ask a waiter to bring us coffee and something Tenny likes for her to nibble on," Jane said quietly.

"Tenny, we're so sorry about your uncle," Shelley said when they were seated.

"Thanks. He was dying, I guess you should know."

"Oh?" Shelley said.

Tenny repeated pretty much what Linda Moosefoot had told them about Bill Smith's poor health, but they didn't let on that they had heard it before. "But nothing could have prepared us for the idea that someone might kill him. My God! It's unbelievable!" she said.

"Who do you think did it?" Jane asked bluntly.

"I have no idea. None! I can still hardly take in the fact that it happened."

"How's your aunt Joanna taking it?" Shelley asked.

"Oh, extraordinarily well. She's quite an amazing woman. She's really observing Uncle Bill's wishes."

"Which were?" Jane asked.

"That his death be ignored as much as possible," Tenny said with a wry smile.

"Ignored?"

"He insisted that there be absolutely no fuss when he went. No funeral service or anything. He and Joanna had talked it all out. He'll be cremated, his ashes scattered by Joanna alone wherever and whenever she chooses. He said, rather contemptuously, I must say—that if we felt we just *had* to have some kind of memorial service, it could be with the tribe, and not any sooner than a month after his death. This is all written out and in a notebook with his will and trust documents."

"Oh, good. He did have that all set up," Shelley said.

"Of course," Tenny said. "It was his way. Very businesslike."

"I hate to be tactless," Jane said, "but could his arrangements have anything to do with his death? I

mean, perhaps he was leaving some bequest to someone who felt they couldn't wait."

"I have no idea what the terms are," Tenny said.
"I'm certain, though, that virtually everything must
go directly to Joanna. And there's probably some
bank or lawyer or someone designated to oversee the
financial aspects of it all. Joanna's not stupid by any
means, but she just hasn't the interest in the business
details that he had. I'm positive he'll have made sure
she doesn't have to be bothered with keeping track of
every penny. I've tried not to pry. In fact, Aunt
Joanna's meeting with the lawyer right now, which is
why I'm sort of at loose ends instead of sitting with
her. Not that she'd probably let me anyway. Claims
she's going to her bridge club meeting Monday just
as if nothing's happened."

"He wouldn't leave those details to Pete? Make
him cotrustee or something?" Shelley asked.

"Oh, God! Never!" Tenny thought for a minute. "I
hadn't thought about that yet. Pete considers himself
to be a financial whiz—he's a failed stockbroker—
and is probably going to be pissed as hell to realize
he's out of the loop. At least I assume he's out of the
loop. I really can't imagine Uncle Bill trusting him
with any decision-making powers. He wouldn't even
give him the authority to order the chemicals for the
swimming pools unless he countersigned the order
form."

"What do you suppose happens to the estate after
your aunt is gone?" Jane asked.

Even Shelley looked mildly shocked that Jane
would ask something that was so clearly none of their
business, but Jane had guessed correctly that Tenny

was just thinking about all this herself for the first time and was too preoccupied to take offense.

"I don't know," she said. "I suppose it'll mostly go to some charity or other since they don't have any children. Maybe a little something for Pete and me."

A waiter appeared with coffee and a plate of little crustless sandwiches, then tactfully disappeared.

"Would he leave anything to the Holnagrad Society?" Shelley asked. "Or the tribe?"

"The tribe, maybe. The Society, no, I don't think so. He considered them pretty much of a harmless nuisance."

"Speaking of Pete and the tribe," Jane said, sensing that Tenny was bound to realize soon that she was talking to strangers about personal matters, "you said he and HawkHunter got into a fight?"

Tenny's eyes flashed. "Yes, the asses! Right out in front of the hotel!"

Jane heard the whine of the shuttle-bus engine as the vehicle came up the last bit of hill. "Shelley, I'll be right back. I want to see if the kids are on this bus." She gave her friend a look that said, *Find out all you can,* and left.

There wasn't anybody familiar on the bus, and when Jane returned, they either had moved on from the subject of the fight or hadn't covered it at all. Jane couldn't help but notice that more than half of the little sandwiches were gone, and there weren't any crumbs anywhere near Shelley. This didn't necessarily prove anything, however, as Shelley was an almost crumb-less eater—a trait Jane didn't really hold against her most of the time.

"Jane, Tenny was telling me about her pottery business," Shelley said.

"Well, not so much a business as a paying hobby," Tenny demurred. "I was looking forward to doing it full-time if Uncle Bill sold the resort."

"You sell your work, then?"

"Here in the gift shop and at several shops in Vail, Frisco, Georgetown, places like that. I've had several upscale catalog suppliers approach me, but my work with the hotel takes up too much of my time to assume that responsibility."

"The gift shop?" Jane exclaimed. "The big serving bowl with the blue-and-green pattern? Is that your work? I've drifted by and admired it several times already. It's absolutely beautiful. That lobelia blue is my favorite color."

"I have a set of six serving bowls to match being fired."

"Oh, stop. I'm going to start drooling in a minute."

Shelley had been listening quietly. "Tenny, I probably shouldn't even be talking about this, but since you've brought up the pottery business—no, never mind."

"What?"

"Well, you realize it's my husband involved with the investors, and I don't mean to jeopardize anybody's position, so don't answer if you don't feel like it—but why are you talking like you can't do your pottery? Doesn't Joanna want to sell the resort? I don't mean right away, understand—"

Tenny took a long sip of her coffee and gestured at the remaining sandwiches. "Please finish these. I'm full." Then she said to Shelley, "I don't mind answering that. It's just my own guess, but I don't think Aunt Joanna will want to sell now. She loathed Florida. Said it was too hot and buggy and full of old people. She's lived all her married life right here, and the whole of her life within a couple miles. Frankly, I think she'll find running the resort, even with advisors, a terrible burden, but it *is* her home. She only went along with the retirement idea because it was what Uncle Bill wanted. I don't mean she was being spineless or martyred, but she really enjoyed making him happy, and getting away from here would have made him very happy."

Shelley thought for a moment, hesitated, then plunged forward. "Tenny, I can't speak for the investors, you understand, only as a concerned friend. But it would seem quite possible that Joanna could at least try to sell the resort on condition that she could stay right where she is for as long as she wanted. Some sort of nominal rent could be computed into the deal, couldn't it? I thought things like that were done all the time. And if it's part of the contract, it would be a legal obligation that got passed right along even if the place were later sold to someone else."

For the first time since they had started talking, Tenny looked almost cheerful.

"You could be right. That's really worth looking into. Oh, I feel so guilty about this, but in the back of my mind I've been so upset—so *selfishly* upset—because Uncle Bill died before he could sell the place and relieve me of my responsibility to it. But if Aunt Joanna could stay and be happy, and if I could stay nearby and keep an eye on her, but live my own life—oh, that would really be wonderful! Do you think it would be appropriate for you to ask your husband if it's a possibility?"

"I'd be happy to," Shelley said. "I'll be speaking to him later today when he gets home."

It had been Jane's turn to keep quiet, and she'd been using the time to wolf down two of the little sandwich triangles, but she had a question bubbling up—well, two questions really, though asking for the recipe for the sandwich filling could wait. "Tenny, do you think other people knew about your aunt's attitude? That she didn't want to move away?"

"Why do you ask?"

"I was just thinking it might have something to do with your uncle's death."

"You mean somebody killed him to keep the resort from being sold?"

"Something like that."

Tenny thought for a minute. "I'm not sure. Pete should have known, if he ever paid attention to what other people think, but he doesn't. If it doesn't directly concern him, it just doesn't seem to register. And I suppose all her old friends must have known."

"Friends in the tribe?"

"Uh-huh. Mostly."

"Friends who might have told HawkHunter?"

Tenny and Shelley both looked at her questioningly.

"Do you mean you suspect HawkHunter of killing my uncle?" Tenny asked.

"Not really. I was just thinking out loud. The fact is, *somebody* killed your uncle. And it could have been almost anyone."

"But if he was killed out in those woods, it *really* could have been anyone at all. Some passing maniac," Tenny said. "Somebody who didn't even know him."

"But how likely is that?" Jane asked. "We're hardly in the middle of an urban center. If he died near where he was found, it was a long way from the road. Your passing maniac would have to park the car, go around behind the resort, walk halfway up a long hill—"

"My God!" Tenny said. "I guess you're right. I just haven't had the time or wits to think this out properly. There aren't people casually passing by out there. Only guests and employees and people from the tribe."

And the mysterious skier, Jane said to herself. Then, to them: "The mysterious skier!"

"What are you talking about?" Tenny asked.

"I've seen him a couple times. Shelley, you saw him this morning, remember?"

"I have no idea what you're going on about," Shelley said bluntly.

"It's somebody I've seen on that slope a few times. No, not on the slope. At the top of the hill a couple times and once coming through the woods. This person, I think it's a man, or maybe a very tall woman, looked like a nature nut. Binoculars, cameras, a notepad. A couple times I've seen him stop and take pictures or look over the resort."

"So you're casting this mystery person as the murderer?" Shelley asked.

"No, not necessarily. But as a possible witness."

"Oh," Shelley said softly. "You could be right. You should tell the sheriff."

"I think I'll mention it to Mel. I've talked quite enough to that sheriff for my lifetime."

"Thanks for making me sit down and eat, and thanks even more for letting me talk," Tenny said, folding her napkin. "I really should get back and see how Aunt Joanna is doing."

"Tenny, feel free to drop in on us anytime you want to get away from everything," Shelley said. "And I'll pass what we talked about on to Paul as soon as I hear from him."

"You know," Tenny mused, "it's been really therapeutic to talk to someone who didn't know Uncle Bill well and can speak calmly and listen dispassionately. Thanks again for letting me bend your ears." She signaled to the waiter, signed the tab with the notation "House Acct.—TG," and left.

"Jane, gulp down the last of your coffee and let's go watch for the kids out in front," Shelley said.

"Did you get her to tell you about the fistfight?"

"Yes, but I'd rather scoop up the kids and go back to our cabin to talk."

──── 15 ────

Shelley and Jane sat down on one of the benches flanking the front doors. It was a sunny afternoon and the benches were warm. Although the women were surrounded by snow, the spot was protected by the wind and was surprisingly comfortable.

"Tell me what Tenny said about the fight," Jane said, as there was nobody else near them at the moment.

"Tenny said she'd come up here to get some paperwork her aunt had asked for and to tactfully avoid being around while the lawyer was visiting. I'm not sure how much of this was from what she actually saw and how much is what people told her. There were a handful of people waiting for the shuttle. Right here, I assume. Pete and HawkHunter ran into each other—Pete coming out, HawkHunter going in. They talked for a few minutes, then their voices got louder and angrier, and suddenly Pete threw a punch that caught HawkHunter right in the chops. Pete spun around and walked off before HawkHunter could even get up. A couple of the people waiting for the shuttle helped him to his feet and tried to tend to his injuries, but he refused—quite nastily, I believe—to let anyone do anything for him. Some talk about the patronizing charity of whites. He stomped off in the other direction. That's the gist of it."

"Was he hurt badly?"

Shelley shook her head. "Apparently not. Dr. Lucke was out here and told Tenny that HawkHunter had a tooth knocked out and a bloody lip and that was about all. Dr. Lucke offered to take a look and recommended immediate treatment—well, he is a dentist, after all—but HawkHunter brushed him off and wouldn't even let him look at his mouth."

"What did the argument sound like it was about?"

A family, all togged out in matching ski outfits and looking like a set of Russian nesting dolls, was approaching so Shelley fell silent until they'd passed with the sort of cheerful greetings people normally employ only while on vacation.

When they'd gone inside, she answered. "Tenny said it was an all-purpose slanging match. HawkHunter said something critical of Bill, and Pete said couldn't the family be left alone to grieve in peace, and HawkHunter said something about respecting the Indian dead, and Pete said something else about his uncle dying so recently. Then HawkHunter launched into a tirade about the racism of it all."

"Huh?"

"That all the Indian dead on the top of the hill didn't matter so long as the greedy white man got his money. That members of the tribe had been living and dying here for centuries before Bill and his kind came to rape the land, and what was one more dead white man?"

"My gosh, I think I'd have taken a swing at him,

too! Even if he's right, it was the wrong time to go on about it."

"Yeah, you can't help but sympathize with Pete."

"Still—"

"What are you thinking?" Shelley asked.

"I guess I'm really getting cynical, but my first thought was that the argument might have been staged. And because they're both rather emotional, it just got out of hand."

"Why would they stage it?"

"I don't know exactly. But look at it this way: HawkHunter was giving Bill Smith a lot of grief. Demonstrating in front of the hotel. Trying to scare off the investors. And remember yesterday morning, how upset Pete was when we met him? That was when the demonstration was going on. Then last night at dinner, there were Pete and HawkHunter, chummy as could be, eating together. Then Bill's found dead today and they're back to being enemies. There's something weird about it all."

"You could be right, of course. But it's also possible that Pete is genuinely unraveled by his uncle's death. Tenny said he was already quite upset about Doris, who was only an acquaintance. And then to have his uncle not only die, but be murdered? That's enough to make anybody damned touchy."

"Especially if he's afraid of being found to have caused one or both deaths," Jane said.

"Do you really think so?" Shelley asked.

Jane shrugged. "I have no idea. I only know that I had nothing to do with either one and there's a dim-bulb good-ol'-boy sheriff who would dearly love to blame it on me. Even if Doris's death is questionable,

Bill Smith was clearly murdered and *somebody* did it. Somebody other than me!"

"But you know we keep coming back to Pete because he's not very likable. It's always easier to believe the worst about someone who's a jerk to begin with."

"True enough, but that's not the only reason. He's obviously playing some complex game of his own, genuinely upset with HawkHunter and the tribe in the morning, palling around with him by the same evening."

"Now, Jane, be fair. He doesn't strike me as a rocket-scientist-caliber brain, but he might have really been trying, in his own way, to represent his uncle's best interests. And for that matter, we don't even know that he's as stupid as he looks. It's entirely possible to look like an overage surfer and still have an I.Q. higher than a kitchen appliance."

Jane laughed. "Tenny doesn't seem to think so."

"But we don't really know Tenny. We never met her until yesterday."

"True," Jane admitted. "Though I sure wouldn't want to have any reason to think badly of her. I really like her."

"She could have some agenda of her own. Jealousy, maybe. We've made most of our judgments about Pete based on things she's said about him. She could be a pathological liar for all we know."

"I'd hate to think so."

"So would I, because I really like her, too, and I'm inordinately proud of my ability to sum people up accurately. But anything's possible."

They could hear the shuttle bus coming up the last

hill and were pleased to see Mike get off it. "Where are the girls, do you know?" Jane asked him.

"They'll probably be on the next bus. They were waiting at the stop with me, but there was something wrong with something they bought and they went back to exchange it."

"Did you have fun skiing today?" Jane asked.

"Yeah, it was okay. But I think I've had enough. I'm tired and sore."

"I'm sort of glad to hear that," Jane said. She explained to him briefly about the resort owner's mysterious death. "Somebody killed him, Mike."

"That's awful!"

"It is. Fortunately, it has nothing to do with us," she said, omitting any mention of her having found the body or the sheriff's apparent suspicions of her. "But the fact is, somebody around here is dangerous. I can't imagine that this person would take the slightest interest in any of us, but—"

"You want me to keep a close eye on Todd and John, right?"

Jane nodded. "I'm going to have my hands full making sure your sister and Denise aren't wandering around on their own."

"The boys won't get out of my sight, Mom. Where are they now?"

"Locked up in the cabin with Mel, who's probably heard enough Super Mario music to last him the rest of his life."

"I'll go up there now. He's probably locked himself in a closet by now. I can just see it. Mel in a fetal position, humming Nintendo music and looking stoned."

"Shelley, why don't you let Mike walk you back?" Jane said. "I'll wait for the girls."

There wouldn't be another shuttle for fifteen minutes, so Jane used the time to run down to the gift shop. She bought the bowl she and Tenny had talked about, even though it was far more than she could afford and would be a challenge to pack. Then she ran to the tiny bookstore and inquired whether it had HawkHunter's book.

"You mean the first one?" the elderly bookstore lady said.

"I guess so. I didn't know he wrote another."

"Oh, yes. The publisher tried to cash in on the success of *I, HawkHunter* and got him to write another. It was a dismal flop. Written too fast, with not much more to say. Just a careless rehash of the best-seller, really. Publishers never learn. It was remaindered about as fast as it was printed."

"My, but you know a lot about it."

"I had a chain of small independent bookstores in Denver back then. I retired up here and run this one just to keep my hand in. This is the last copy until I get another order," she added, taking a paperback copy from the rack to the left of the counter.

"I'm surprised you carry his book here."

"Why is that?"

"Well, he's not exactly a friend of the resort."

"Oh, the Smiths wouldn't think of interfering in my stock. That's our agreement. And he is a celebrity. I don't think they care anyway. Half the people who have bought copies since yesterday thought the demonstration was some kind of free entertainment."

Jane was back in her spot in front of the resort when the next shuttle arrived. She was relieved to see

Katie and Denise on board, not least of all because she was no longer in the fading sunshine and it was getting uncomfortably cold. They got off the shuttle urging her to look at their purchases—a lot of hair paraphernalia, primarily. "Come on, girls, I want to go back to the cabin," Jane told them.

"Were you waiting for us?" Katie asked suspiciously.

"I'm afraid so. Let's go. I'll explain why on the way."

Jane gave them an even more abbreviated version of what she'd told Mike. "Now, I don't want to frighten you. There's no need to be worried. As long as you're in our cabin with the doors locked or in the lodge, there's no question that you're entirely safe. And we're all probably safe anyplace else, too. But just to be real sure, I don't want you going back and forth without an adult."

"Oh, Mom! We're not *babies!*" Katie said. But Jane recognized this as an obligatory whine. Much the teenage equivalent of the perfect housekeeper who automatically laments what a mess the house is when visitors come.

"I guess you've been eating all afternoon?" she asked, to change the subject as they started up the road. "There's a dance here tonight, but it isn't until eight o'clock. I thought we might rest for a while, maybe nibble some of the stuff we've got at the cabin, then come down here for dinner."

"What kind of dance?" Denise asked.

"A line dance, the poster said. Whatever that is."

The girls groaned in unison.

"That bad?" Jane asked. "We'll give it a try anyhow. Nobody from home is around to know. And it might be fun. And there might be some interesting boys there."

The girls considered this in silence for the rest of the way.

Shelley was sound asleep when they got back. The girls disappeared into their own room and closed the door. Jane started a pot of coffee and tidied up the living room. While doing so, she discovered to her annoyance that she still had Doris Schmidtheiser's file folder. She'd have to remember to give it to Lucky, who could return it to Doris's family or offer it to a member of the Holnagrad Society who might want to continue her research. Jane sat down and took the papers out, mildly curious. They were still in a jumble, just as they had been when she'd picked them up and stuffed them in the folder. She sorted them into stacks of similar-looking documents.

Most of it didn't make any sense at all to her. There were copies of old census reports which were interesting in a purely historical sense. She liked the look of the old-fashioned handwriting and found the sizes of the families on the sheets interesting, if appalling. Most of the families seemed to have a child every two years like clockwork. Here and there was a three-year gap, which Jane took to indicate a miscarriage or a stillborn baby. Many of the women were in their forties and still had an infant around, as well as children as old as the early twenties. Jane tried for a moment to imagine herself with a tiny baby and a couple more still to come, and shuddered at the thought.

There were also a great many middle-aged spin-

sters and bachelors living with elderly parents, sometimes several in a family. It was hard to realize that
marriage hadn't always been the norm. A man who
couldn't support a family simply didn't marry. And a
woman who never got a proposal had no alternative
but to stay at home forever. Jane found herself studying these long-dead families and imagining their
lives. It was surprising how much you could tell
about a different way of life just from names, ages,
and the other seemingly impersonal data on the
forms. On one sheet, depicting a New York neighborhood at the turn of the century, not a single adult
listed his or her place of birth as anywhere in the
United States. On a single street there were Rileys,
O'Callahans, Kolenskis, Kleinschmids, McSheas,
Pfeiffers, and Joneses. What a rich jumble of lan-
guages one must have heard spoken along the side-
walks there!

After a bit, Jane folded up the census reports and
put them in a pile, then began looking over the rest
of the contents of the file. There were a lot of newspaper clippings, some originals protected in plastic
sleeves, some photocopies. Most had to do with the
Romanovs. One very old one was a small official
portrait of Tsar Nicholas and a cousin Sergei not long
before the Tsar had abdicated, according to the text
of the article, which was from a London newspaper.
Perhaps this man was the father of the Gregor Roman
that Doris had followed. There was a much larger du-
plicate of this picture in the folder as well. It was also
much clearer—apparently a copy of the actual photograph. On the back was a handwritten notation of
where and when the photo had been taken, and the

name of a person in Holnagrad. Presumably this was who had supplied it to Doris.

Jane set the clippings on the pile as well. All the rest of the material was handwritten and typed notes. Many of these had to do with Gregory Smith of Colorado. One sheet, a handwritten one, was a sort of chart. It was labeled "Sheepshead Bay Court Records," with a long film number and three columns. Two names were starred with a red pen:

*Roman, G.	Book B	page 16
Dolman, T.	Book B	page 601
*Smith, N.D.	Book D	page 493
Smith, A.C.	Book G	page 83
Rutheven, ?	Book M	page 500
Wiley, J.	Book O	page 4
Aulkunder, J.	Book Y	page 342
Sellinger, Q.	Book Y	page 770
Schellberger, ?	Book Z	page 113
Harmon, D.	Book AA	page 612

What on earth was this all about? Jane wondered. Were all these people somehow connected with Gregory Smith? At least in Doris's mind they must have been. The references must have to do with documents, but what kind of documents? The list would surely mean something to somebody who knew how to translate it.

Satisfied that she'd tidied up the file, Jane slipped everything back into the folder and put it on the counter between the kitchen and the dining area. She must remember to give it to Lucky so that it could go to someone to whom it would mean something. She poured herself a cup of coffee, took it back to the living room, and stretched out on one of the sofas to skim through her new copy of *I, HawkHunter*.

That was where Shelley found her an hour later, sound asleep with the book over her face like a tent.

16

"Jane, wake up. The sheriff wants to talk to you," Shelley hissed.

Jane sat up, angry with herself for falling asleep and feeling so fuddled. "Give me a minute to slap myself awake," she said, tearing toward the bathroom, where she slapped some cold water on her face and brushed her teeth fiercely, thinking at least her gums and cheeks would be awake and they were both fairly close to her brain.

As it turned out, she didn't need any special wits for this interview. The sheriff asked her the same things he'd already asked before. Did she know Doris or Bill before coming here? Was she a member of the group that was meeting here? Why did she go to Mrs. Schmidtheiser's cabin? Why did she head toward the snowman? This was a new one and it made Jane laugh, which the sheriff clearly found a distasteful reaction. "I wasn't 'heading' for anything! It was the first time I ever skied and I had absolutely no control over where I ended up! Do you really imagine I'd have risked running into a tree or something by heading for the woods?"

"I couldn't say. I just couldn't say, ma'am. But it sure is odd that there's two bodies and somebody

157

who says she never knew the people before found both of them, don't you think?"

This was at least the third time he'd made this observation. The first time it had surprised her, the second time it irritated her, but this time—in her own temporary "home" and with her daughter in the next room—it made her furious.

"Are you making an accusation?" she said coldly.

"No, ma'am. Nosiree. Just sayin' as how it's odd."

She stood up and walked to the door of the cabin. "It was unpleasant and unfortunate. And I find this conversation to be even more so. I've told you everything I know. And I've told it to you several times. If you have in mind asking me the same questions again, you'll have to ask them of my lawyer. Frankly, I'm tired of this. Get out of here."

"Now, don't go gettin' all riled up—"

"Get out!"

He put his hands up. "Okay, okay, I'm going." He backed out the door, making vaguely apologetic noises, but Jane cut them off by slamming the door as soon as he was outside. She leaned back against it, shaking.

Shelley looked at her admiringly. "Wow! I've never seen you do anything like that. I'm really impressed!"

"You're rubbing off on me, I guess. That ignorant, nasty-minded hick! How dare he—"

"Now calm down. He's gone."

A few minutes and a restorative cup of coffee and cigarette later, Shelley ventured to reopen the subject. "You see what this means, don't you?"

"I have no idea," Jane said.

"Look, the people here are bright and much more

sophisticated than they like to let on. They wouldn't have anybody as sheriff who really is as much of a rube as he acts like. So he must be smarter than he seems."

"He'd have to be!"

"And if he has the wits to stay sheriff, he must know you're telling the truth."

"Rave on," Jane said. "So why is he bothering with me?"

"Because he's at a dead end."

"Are you suggesting that I should be encouraged by this?"

"Not encouraged, but it does mean there isn't any evidence that we don't know about that's helping him any. So we are just as well equipped to figure this out as he is."

"And just as motivated," Jane added sourly.

"Okay, so we can assume that either both deaths have to do with the whole Tsar/Holnagrad thing or they don't."

"That's a big help."

"Jane, it gives us a structure for analyzing what we know."

"If you say so."

"All right. Let's assume first that it does have to do with the Tsar business. Which certainly seems likely, since one death was the person promoting Bill Smith as the heir, and the other death was Bill himself."

"Okay, I see where you're going now," Jane said. "Who are the people involved in any way? Pro or con?"

"Right. There are the two victims, of course. There's Pete, and we've already talked about him pretty thoroughly. There's Stu Gortner, who is really the one with the greatest motivation to get rid of the competition for his candidate."

"Wait—go back to Pete. What would this fight he got into with HawkHunter have to do with it?"

"Hold it, Jane. Don't sidetrack me yet. We're just laying out the groundwork for how we're going to think about this."

"So we're thinking about how we're going to think? You wouldn't like to offer to run a couple states and several major corporations in your spare time, would you?"

Shelley ignored that remark. "So—we have Bill, Doris, Pete, and Stu as interested parties. Now we have to add Joanna. Don't make faces like that. Joanna's very much a concerned party. Suppose Doris had made some kind of grand announcement to the press about Bill being the rightful Tsar. On Bill's behalf as well as her own, that would have a real impact on her life."

"Okay, I'll give you that."

"We've also got to consider Lucky. He's the president of the Society and had both Doris and Stu trying to get him on their sides. Maybe he is quietly involved with one or the other of them."

"But that could be true of practically anyone in the Society."

"Yes, but the rest of them don't appear to have much of anything at stake. Stu sees his candidate as his way to fame and fortune. Same with Pete. Doris saw it as a private coup. Even Lucky, who seems to care deeply about the Society, may feel that the group itself could either triumph or dissolve in the publicity a 'new Tsar' would generate."

"I notice you're not mentioning Tenny."

"No. Except that Tenny didn't want her uncle bothered with it, I can't see a motive for her. Even if she did have a motive to knock off Doris to protect Bill, she'd hardly hurt Bill. So there are the suspects *if* it has to do with the Holnagrad Society."

"What else could it logically have to do with?"

"The sale of the resort, for one thing."

"You suspect Paul!"

"Jane, quit being silly."

"I'm sorry."

"Since the two deaths occurred so close together and right now, I think we have to assume that something in particular precipitated them. Nobody around here is a drooling maniac, so you have an otherwise normal person who has to do something terrible immediately for some reason."

"To keep the sale from going through, maybe," Jane said, nodding. "Or to make sure it does go through. The great problem is Doris. I can't imagine that there's any way that Doris's death would make the slightest difference either way."

"Unless Doris's death was suicide."

"Come on!"

"I know it seems absurd, but it is possible. Jane, we don't know anything whatsoever of her background. For all we know, she could have lived half her life in mental institutions. It's not likely, but it could be that the humiliation of that debate drove her over the edge. On the other hand, we know absolutely that Bill's death was a murder. So let's deal with him for a minute. A handful of people had a stake in the sale of the resort. Joanna again—Bill's death allows her to avoid Florida."

"It also makes her a widow."

Shelley shrugged. "Maybe she wanted to be a widow. A rich widow. Just because she crochets the ugliest afghans west of the Piedmont doesn't mean she might not have simply snapped and said to herself, 'I can't stand another day with this man!' Wives have felt that way before. And Pete has any number of possible motives here, too. Bill and Joanna have no children. He and Tenny are their logical heirs. That makes them both suspects."

"But Joanna's still alive. And she's sure to inherit everything."

"According to Tenny, I remind you. Even if she does inherit everything, either Pete or Tenny might have thought they could put something over on her that they couldn't put over on Bill, who could apparently hang onto his money extraordinarily well."

"Are we still just thinking about thinking, or may I speculate?"

"Not yet. If the sale of the resort is the reason for Bill's death, we also have to consider HawkHunter."

"Oh, good. I like him as a suspect."

"Jane!"

"I didn't mean that quite as smart-alecky as it sounded. Sorry. But he is the sort of person who thrives on rousing people's emotions. A catalyst type. Maybe not directly responsible, but the person who makes other people act. Like goading Pete into punching him. Maybe he goaded Pete into killing his uncle. Think about him for a minute while I refill our coffee."

"No more for me, thanks."

When Jane got back, Shelley was deep in thought. "I don't know about HawkHunter. I see what you mean about goading people, but what about a motive of his own?"

"He's a fanatic," Jane said.

"But lots of people are fanatics about one thing or another. That doesn't make them murderers."

"What I meant is, this sale touched on his fanaticism. The tribal graves up on the hill. He could have really believed that the graves were safe from desecration only as long as Bill owned the land, because Bill respected the tribe—oops. I just proved he wouldn't murder Bill, didn't I? No, let me think. Bill was set on selling the land. Maybe HawkHunter learned from Joanna's friends in the tribe that she probably wouldn't want to sell out and leave if Bill died first. How's that?"

Shelley shook her head. "It's still just a matter of time. Joanna won't live forever. Someday the land will be sold. If not now, then later."

"But it might have been time he needed. Maybe he felt that if he only had another six months or whatever, he could prove the graves were up there. Or prove there was something illegal about the original land grant."

Shelley nodded, but without enthusiasm. "I guess that's possible."

The phone rang. "Hi, Mel," Jane said after she'd answered it.

"Are we going to dinner and the big dance? Or is it canceled because of Bill's death?"

"Oh, I'm sure Joanna has insisted that it *not* be canceled. Have you managed to learn anything more?"

"A few useless bits and pieces. We'll talk about it

at dinner, okay? Can you be ready in fifteen minutes?"

"Sure," she said, glancing in a nearby mirror at her nap-crumpled hair and thinking, *No way!*

"Say, Janey, I hate to mention this, but I'm starting to wonder if this thin air is doing something to Mike's brain. When he came in this afternoon, he suddenly burst into laughter for no reason at all, then wouldn't explain it."

"What were you doing when he came in?" Jane asked, suspicious.

"Just looking around on the floor of the closet for a missing sock. Why?"

"You weren't humming anything, were you?" She giggled. "Never mind. I'll explain later."

She hung up. "Shelley, talk fast. Mel's on his way over. Girls!" she yelled down the hallway. "We're leaving in a few minutes. Get ready."

"Okay," Shelley said, gathering up cups and saucers and setting them in the sink. "The third possibility, which I mention only for form's sake, is that the death or deaths have nothing to do with anything we know about."

"A ripe field of inquiry," Jane said. "Are we finally through getting ready to think?"

"I believe so."

"So when do we do the real thinking?"

"Oh," Shelley said airily, "we'll let our collective subconscious work on that while we eat dinner. First dibs on the bathroom."

—— 17 ——

Mel and the boys arrived shortly, and while they all
waited with varying degrees of impatience for Katie
and Denise to get ready, the boys took Willard outside for a run in the snow. "Poor old Willard," Jane
said. "He knows how to pee downwind in a Chicago
gale, but he can't figure out how to manage with
snow up to his shoulders."

"That's one of the many things I've always admired about Willard," Mel said. "That peeing-
downwind trick."

"What did you learn from the sheriff?" Jane asked,
ignoring the sarcasm.

"Nothing of any real use," Mel admitted. "There's
no question, of course, of finding footprints. For one
thing, it had snowed lightly after the snowman was
built, and that pretty well obliterated any marks. And
by the time you, half the skiers, and all the police had
stumbled around, there was no hope left."

"I wouldn't think snow would hold footprints anyway: Up here in the mountains, it's so powdery that
the least wind must make it move around like sand,"
Shelley said. "What else?"

"Plinkbarrel, or whatever his damned name is, says
there were wool fibers in the snow that had been

165

packed around the body. From mittens, he speculated. They didn't match anything the victim was wearing."

"Ah! That sounds helpful," Jane said.

Mel shook his head. " 'Fraid not. The sheriff, or more likely one of his minions, checked out the stuff in that lost-and-found room and discovered the mittens there. Still damp. And the insides of fuzzy wool mittens won't hold fingerprints, I'm sorry to say."

Jane thought for a minute. "Doesn't that imply premeditation? I mean, a deliberate plan to murder him, not just a momentary rage? Before murdering Bill, somebody took the mittens that couldn't be traced to himself or herself and then returned them later."

"Possibly. But not for certain. The perp may have borrowed the mittens for no purpose at all except warmth, then recovered his or her wits enough to put them back. For that matter, they might not have even come from the lost-and-found originally. They might have belonged to the murderer, who just figured that was a good way of disposing of them without being caught with them in his possession. I wouldn't think anybody keeps track of every mitten in that room. It's just a hodgepodge that probably gets culled only once each spring."

"But that does limit it to people with knowledge of the hotel," Jane said.

"I guess it does," Mel admitted. "But I don't think that was ever in doubt."

"Where did the other stuff come from?" Shelley asked. "That bowl thing that was the crown, and the whatever-it-was that looked like a robe?"

"The bowl is one that's in a lot of the cabins. A local firm delivers fruit gift packs in them," Mel said. "They're usually left in the cabins. And the robe was just a standard-issue blanket—one of the extras that are in the closet of each cabin. Unfortunately, they get shifted around, too. Family groups like this one move around, people get cold and use a blanket like a shawl to run back to their own cabins, and so forth. They only get sorted out if the maids happen to notice that there's an excess in one cabin and a shortage in another."

"None of which is any help at all," Jane said.

"Unless the sheriff knows a lot he's not telling me. Which is possible," Mel replied.

"And what did he say about me?" Jane asked, then added, "Never mind," as the boys and Willard came back in. She certainly didn't want the kids to know she was under suspicion, however absurd the idea was.

Katie and Denise were eventually dragged away from their bathroom, where they were still feverishly consulting on makeup, and the whole mob moved off toward the lodge. Mel went ahead with the kids, who were engaged in a traveling snowball fight. The snow was so cold and dry that it was hard to form into a ball at all, and most of them exploded into powder before ever reaching a target.

"It must have been hard to build a snowman," Shelley speculated.

Jane nodded. "I think that was the reason for the blanket/robe thing. So the back didn't have to be covered. Maybe you have to pour water on snow to make it hold its shape here. To form a crust. That's probably why you don't see many snowmen."

"I don't suppose the sheriff is likely to confide in us whether that was done," Shelley said. "But it could be significant. You'd have to have some kind of thermos along."

"I don't think that would be much help in narrowing down suspects, though," Jane said. "Lots of people carry around thermoses. They even sell them in the equipment hut with a sort of belt-loop thing so you can hang it onto yourself somewhere. I noticed because it looked like a good way to carry coffee."

"You're right. I'd thought of that, too, but had forgotten."

"But there's something we've kind of overlooked about this," Jane remarked. "The fact that the snowman was gotten up to look—well, *regal*. Doesn't that mean Bill's death had something to do with the Tsar thing?"

"Not necessarily. You said yourself the robe thing was probably a device to save somebody from having to cover the body all the way around."

"True, but there was the crown, too. There was no practical purpose for that. Nor for the old bent ski pole the snowman was holding in its stick arms that looked like a scepter. Doesn't all of that look like deliberate mockery of the whole concept of Bill Smith as Tsar?"

"Unless the motive was completely unrelated and the murderer just did that to make it look like the genealogists were guilty in some way."

"Jeez, Shelley! If a murderer were really that clever, he'd have thought of a better way to solve his problem than to kill Mr. Smith—and maybe Mrs. Schmidtheiser, too."

"You'd think so, but that's because we haven't got what a murderer has—a conscience, or lack of conscience, that even allows the *thought* of murder as a solution to a problem."

"Yes, but it still seems most likely that the whole 'royal trimmings' business does point to the Holnagrad/Tsar situation."

"I agree it's very likely," Shelley allowed. "But where does that get us?"

"I dunno," Jane said wearily. She suddenly realized she was sick and tired of the whole business. She'd come here for a long-awaited and well-deserved vacation and—dammit!—she was going to have fun—if it killed her.

The Saturday night dinner and dance *were* fun.

The casual dining room had been set up with a stupendous Tex-Mex buffet. Jane planned to sample a tiny bit of everything, but couldn't get through half of her testing. Not only was there a huge variety, but she found a casserole dish called King Ranch Chicken that she fell so much in love with that she had three helpings.

"I'm going to get this recipe if I have to beat up the chef to make him reveal it," she exclaimed. "Try it, Shelley. It tastes sort of plum-blossomish."

"It must have corn tortillas torn up in it," Shelley said, taking a bite from Jane's overloaded plate. "They have that plum-blossom taste. Mmmm. That's wonderful!"

"Glad you think so. You can beat up the chef, then. It's much more your line."

Shelley grinned. "I've never laid violent hands on a chef. Yet. I save that for IRS agents."

It was a festive evening, in spite of the recent death of the resort owner. Jane even noticed Joanna looking in the doorway of the restaurant once, smiling as if genuinely pleased at how well she was managing to implement her husband's last wishes that his death be ignored.

What a strange, strange marriage they'd had, Jane thought. But then, she'd always thought that nearly every marriage, if examined closely enough, would look strange to anyone but the two main participants. Perhaps that was one of the elements that contributed to the increase in the divorce rate, she speculated. Too many people who expected their own marriage to be like what they assumed others were, rather than just accepting the inherent individual weirdnesses of the situation.

She almost mentioned this thought, then decided that discussing marriage in front of Mel might lead him to the erroneous conclusion that she was hinting at something she wasn't.

This led to deeper thoughts. She watched him as he chatted with Shelley and the boys, who had condescended to sit at the same table with the adults. Denise and Katie had, of course, insisted on sitting by themselves at the far end of the room. They were horrified that someone might discover that they had parents. Mel was telling a joke that made Shelley laugh, and Jane stared at his dimple. Would she have been so attracted to him from the first if it weren't for that dimple? she wondered. Of course she would, but maybe not so quickly or wholeheartedly.

The greatest surprise in their relationship had been sex. In her marriage with Steve, sex had been a duty. To be fair, it was a pleasant enough duty most of the time, but still a duty. She had always thought the failure to enjoy it thoroughly and every time was a failing of hers. But since her relationship with Mel had taken an intimate turn, she'd discovered how very wrong she'd been. Steve had simply had no imagination, nor any real awareness of her as an equally important participant. Whereas Mel, who was normally a serious, responsible individual, was as playful and silly as an otter in bed.

Sex with Mel was downright fun. It involved a whole lot of laughter. And he made her completely forget a lot of things she needed to forget: her stretch marks, her own limited experience, and the fact that she was slightly older than he. She might have been locked into domesticity and missed *the* sexual revolution, but she'd certainly had one of her own in the past few months.

So why didn't she want desperately to marry him? She had no idea. It wasn't that she was opposed to the idea of marrying again someday, just that it didn't seem important. No, she wasn't being quite honest with herself. She was opposed. Very slightly. She'd gone from being a daughter to a wife to a mother. She was still a daughter and a mother, but the duties and hazards of those roles were less onerous now than they had once been. But having shed wifeliness, she was becoming quite content.

She was in love with Mel, but she didn't look forward to getting intimately involved in doing his laundry. She wasn't eager to learn what he was like to live with when he had a bad cold. Or was doing his income taxes. Or was trying to fix a lawn mower. She didn't want to have to explain or defend or even talk about her household budget. And while she often consulted with him, as she did with Shelley, about decisions she had to make—things about the kids, or buying a new car, or whether the roof on her house would last another couple years—she didn't really want to have to make those decisions jointly. Decision making, which had scared the daylights out of her when Steve had died, had gone to her head now. She liked it. And intended to hang onto the power it gave her.

"What deep thoughts you must be having," Mel said to her, startling her from her reverie. "We're talking about dessert and you're not even listening. Is something wrong?"

"Nothing at all is wrong," she said, smiling.

The dance was held in the conference room where the genealogy debate had taken place. Jane had been unaware that this room connected to two others by way of big dividers that were open now, making a huge area. A very loud country band was well into its repertoire by the time they arrived. Katie and Denise were already there and had found plenty of companionship. Mike immediately wandered off. The little boys declared that dancing was stupid, and begged to be allowed to spend the evening in the game room. With warnings that they were not to go anywhere else without permission, and with a largish contribution of quarters, they were allowed to leave.

There were tables set up around the entire perimeter of the dance floor with cash bars halfway down each side. Jane, Shelley, and Mel found a vacant table at the far end of the room from the band and settled in. Jane watched the line dancing for a while and reluctantly came to the conclusion that the little boys were right in this case. Line dancing looked stupid and boring to her.

Shelley echoed her thoughts. "This doesn't look

like a cultural trend I'll ever be able to embrace with much enthusiasm," she said thoughtfully. "I understand the appeal of a waltz or a nice, slow, close-together two-step. I can even grasp why people like to polka, and I once was able to do a really mean twist, but this is a sort of down-home version of a conga line. I don't get it."

"We're just frumps," Jane said contentedly.

"Now, now, you ladies are much too young to talk about yourselves that way," a voice said from behind Jane.

"Lucky!" Jane exclaimed. "How nice of you. Will you join us?"

"For a minute or two. My wife parked me here and told me not to get into any trouble," he said with a smile. "As if I'm likely to."

Jane introduced him to Mel, then said, "I keep forgetting to give you something, Lucky. I have a folder that belonged to Mrs. Schmidtheiser. She dropped it when she came out of the debate and ran off before I could give it back to her."

"How long are you staying?"

"We leave at the crack of dawn on Tuesday," Jane replied.

"Good. I'm here through Tuesday, so I'll pick it up from you before you go."

"Just out of curiosity, what will you do with it? The folder and all her other research, for that matter? Did she have any children who might be interested? Or a husband?"

"No, Doris was widowed as a young woman and only had one son, and he isn't remotely interested. I'll probably put it into the Society's library for the time being. That's what I'm doing with the rest of the materials she had with her. And her son has said he'll box up all her research at home and send it on to me as well."

"Poor thing," Shelley said. "To think of all her work just being packed away in boxes like that."

"Oh, it'll be put to use, I'm sure. There's a slightly younger woman in the Society who's worked with her and will probably carry on," Lucky said. "Which may be a mixed blessing."

"Carry on with the Tsar research, you mean?" Jane asked.

"Oh, no, that's not what I was referring to. No. Doris was a professional genealogist. Did a lot of work for other people. Earned a decent living at it. In fact, she moved to Salt Lake City to be able to use the Mormon library without having to wait for films to arrive in Cleveland, where she used to live."

"Why do you say that it's a mixed blessing for someone to carry on her work?" Jane asked.

"I shouldn't tell tales out of school," Lucky replied with mock primness.

"They're the best kind of tales," Shelley assured him. "Do lots of people hire genealogists instead of looking things up themselves?"

"Mobs. Sometimes a person has an assignment from Great-Aunt Maud, who wants the work done, but the person the job is assigned to isn't really interested and would rather pay than do it himself. It's very tedious sometimes, reading through reels and reels of film in the hope of spotting just one familiar name. And then, people who really like doing the work themselves often don't have all the time they need for it, and they'll farm out specific areas of their research to a professional. But Doris—well, Doris wasn't always as 'disinterested' as she might have been."

"You're saying she was a snoop?" Mel surmised. He'd been quietly watching the dancing and hadn't looked like he was even listening to the conversation until now.

Lucky nodded. "Doris was a celebrity hound, to put it bluntly. Years ago she was invited to do a little local talk show, and as a splashy way of showing off, she hunted down a bunch of information on the host of the show and surprised him by tracing his family back to George the Third or somebody. It was a huge hit, word got around, and she got invited to do other shows. It was like getting a taste of blood. She discovered the celebrities have lots of money and not much time, but are often obsessively interested in their own background. She'd actually solicited customers that way, which is frowned on in genealogical circles."

"You mean she'd look up stuff about them, show it to them, and ask if they wanted more, instead of waiting for them to come to her?" Shelley asked.

"Exactly. And it usually worked. The payoff, of course, was that she got to be on first-name terms with famous people, which she loved. The downside of it was, sometimes she'd find stuff they weren't happy to know—illegitimacy and such—or much more often she'd prove they sprang from very common stock. Of course, almost all of us do, but lots of famous people don't like hearing that. Only politicians bother to pretend they like being common. Everybody else secretly wants to be able to brag that they are a cousin of Queen Elizabeth or Albert Einstein."

Jane's mind was clicking along. "Lucky, I hate to ask this, but I must. If she had found out something horrible about someone—"

Mel put his hand on her knee warningly.

"Blackmail!" Shelley breathed.

"I was trying to come up with a more tactful term," Jane chided her.

Mel was shaking his head as if to say, *I tried to head off this discussion.*

Lucky was also shaking his head. "Absolutely not! Not in a million years. The few people who were insulted or angry about her information, and said so, devastated her. She had no judgment about what would offend people, but she positively bristled with moral fiber. She would have been shocked to the core at the very thought of blackmail."

"You're quite certain?" Jane asked.

"I'd literally stake my life on it. God knows Doris had a lot of flaws, but greed for money wasn't one of them. Greed for attention, or for professional recognition, yes. But not for money. In fact, the more rich and famous a client was, the less she'd charge for her work. It was the connection to celebrity that really intoxicated her."

"Speaking of intoxication, would anybody else like a drink?" Mel asked.

—— 18 ——

When the band finally took a break, lowering the noise level, Jane turned to Shelley and asked, "Do you think we can believe him? Lucky, I mean."

Lucky's wife had collected him a few minutes before.

"I think we have to," Shelley said with regret.

"But blackmail would be a nice way of explaining Doris's death."

"I know, but he was so adamant and he knew her very well for years and years. And it's not as if he exactly minded finding fault with her. I think if blackmail was even the most remote possibility, he'd have said so."

"I'm afraid I agree," Jane said reluctantly. "Phooey."

"Besides, it wouldn't connect with Bill Smith's death, even if it were the case."

Jane nodded. "There's Tenny. She's looking for somebody."

Tenny glanced toward them and waved.

"Us, apparently," Shelley said. "I wish she didn't feel like she had to go out of her way to be friendly to us at such a hard time in her own life."

Tenny was weaving her way through the crowd toward them and sat down heavily in the chair Lucky had vacated when she finally reached them. "What a mob!" she said.

"It's a nice turnout," Shelley said. "How are you and your aunt getting along?"

"Fine. Really. Just fine. I'm starting to think Uncle Bill had the right idea. If you force yourself to pretend someone isn't really gone, pretty soon you start believing it. This is about the best crowd we've had for a dance all winter," she added, glancing toward the lines at the cash bars in a professional manner and no doubt doing a little mental calculation of profits. "We might have to try having a second dance night in the middle of the week, too. We used to have bingo games on Wednesday and they were very popular, but the law came down on us."

"Why?" Shelley asked.

"Oh, the gambling laws in Colorado are strict. Of course, we were pretty stupid about it and had no idea anybody really considered bingo as gambling, so we blithely went along for two years with the games until somebody complained."

"But there's a state lottery," Shelley said. "I saw the tickets for sale at the airport."

"Yes, a state lottery, and some nonprofit organizations can play bingo to raise funds. Churches and fraternal organizations and things like that. But we didn't qualify. It's a shame. There could be gigantic profits on real gambling if it was allowed. People who normally wouldn't even buy a lottery ticket at home will throw away all kinds of money when they're on vacation. Anyway, I just wanted to say hello and see how you're all getting along."

"Wonderfully well," Shelley said. "But you

mustn't worry about us. Is there anything we can do for you?"

"No, not really. We're doing fine. At least Aunt Joanna and I are. Pete's in a terrible snit, though."

"Why is that?" Jane asked bluntly.

"Because, as it turns out, I'm cotrustee with Aunt Joanna of Bill's estate. I was surprised, but Pete was horrified. He's gone off in a huff someplace."

"I don't mean to be grim, but are you sure he went off willingly?" Shelley said, tactfully skimming the fact that Tenny had originally thought her uncle Bill had departed of his own volition.

"Yes, I saw him drive off. In fact, he was yelling out the window at me as he went that he was going to find his own lawyer and get me replaced. Don't worry. I shouldn't have mentioned it. He'll cool off and come back. And if he does follow through and succeed in getting rid of me, which he can't, I'd be relieved."

"I talked to my husband very briefly," Shelley said, "and shared your concern about selling with a provision that your aunt could stay here, and he said it would be a breeze. In fact—"

Jane excused herself, feeling that this was a business discussion that wasn't any of her business. She was also wondering what had become of Mel. The last she'd seen of him, he'd volunteered to look for Katie and Denise in the crowd, just to make sure they were still safe and sound. She found him with two very attractive young women who had him more or less pinned in a corner. To give him credit, he didn't look too happy with the arrangement.

"Mel, did you find the girls?" Jane asked.

"Oh, no!" the blond girl with the magnificently

cantilevered bosom said. "I bet you're his wife and I bet we're not the girls you're talking about, huh?!"

Jane started to deny it, but Mel quickly said with dreadful heartiness, "She sure is, and I'm in trouble now. Come on, honey, let's look for the kids!"

"What an extraordinary thing to do," Jane said when he'd briskly steered her across the room and out the door into the hallway.

"My God! They were so aggressive it even scared me. You would have been shocked to hear what they suggested the three of us do. Them and me, that is."

"I'd really rather not know," Jane said.

"By the way, the girls are drinking ginger ale with a bunch of kids up next to the bandstand. I even contrived to 'accidentally' take a sip of Katie's to make real sure it was ginger ale."

"I'll bet you were very subtle about it," Jane said wryly.

"I don't think they noticed," Mel said, aggrieved.

Jane laughed. "Mel, teenage girls are super-finely attuned to any infringement on their imagined adulthood. They can find evidence and take offense at being checked up on even when it's not happening at all. But when it is, you might as well be wearing a sandwich board. Still, it was a nice thought."

He shrugged. "Well, I tried."

Jane slipped her arm around his waist and leaned against him. "It's nice and cool and quiet out here. Let's check on the boys and find some place to sit down for a while. I left Shelley talking business with Tenny. By the way, Tenny said she's cotrustee with her aunt and Pete has gone berserk about it—apparently to the point that he's threatening to get a lawyer to harass her."

"Not good," Mel said.

"Tenny's not too worried. And from the sound of it, I think the sale of the resort will probably go through anyway and Tenny will be relieved of the responsibility for running things." She explained to him about Tenny's pottery and her desire to get on with her own life. She was tempted to speculate on Pete's reaction, whereabouts, and the significance of both on his role as a suspect. But she'd promised herself to enjoy the evening without thinking about the whole thing and firmly put it out of her mind.

"You know, I was so interested in the main courses at dinner that I completely forgot to think about dessert," she said. "I must be sliding right into senility!"

"Then I think we better remedy that," Mel said.

They found the little boys in the game room, which was unfortunate in a way because they'd almost run out of money and Jane had to give them some more; then she and Mel went to the formal dining room, which was nearly empty.

"Is it too late to just have coffee and dessert?" Jane asked the maître d'.

"Not at all," he assured them, leading the way to the Cigar Room, where the same young man who had been there the night before was manning the dessert cart. Linda Moosefoot was the only other customer, and she'd been talking with him when they entered.

"Dance refugees?" she greeted them. She looked a bit tousled herself and Jane thought she remembered seeing Linda fleetingly at the dance. Apparently off-duty employees were welcome to attend, which made Jane like Tenny and Joanna even more.

"Will you join us?" Mel said.

"Sure."

They talked for a while about the dance, Linda's schooling, and the resort. The young man with the dessert cart sat down and joined them as well. It turned out he was Thomas Whitewing, Linda's fiancé. When they'd finished their dessert, he offered Mel a cigar from a wooden box stamped with the resort's logo, which Mel declined.

"I'd sure like a cigarette," Jane said. "Do you have any, Thomas? I bought a pack, but I've lost it somewhere."

"We don't sell them here, but I've got some. Take a couple," he said, pulling a nearly full pack from his back pocket.

"Don't buy another gift-shop pack," Linda said. "I'll pick up some at the general store for you in the morning. They're only forty-five cents a pack."

"You're kidding! How can that be?"

Linda smiled. "One of the benefits of being an Indian. The general store is on the tribe's land. Reservation." When Jane still looked blank, she said, "It's federal land. All reservations are. So we're not subject to state laws and taxation. Cheap cigarettes and no sales tax or property tax. Want just a pack or a carton?"

"A carton is tempting, but it's against my own rules to own more than one full pack at a time. I'm quitting, you see," she added nobly.

"She's been quitting for as long as I've known her," Mel added.

"I haven't seen HawkHunter around tonight," Jane said. "He wasn't hurt seriously in the fight, was he?" She hadn't even realized she was wondering about him until she heard herself inquiring. He must have been quietly batting around in her subconscious for some time.

Linda and her fiancé exchanged quick looks; then Linda said, "Thomas and I don't quite agree about HawkHunter and Little Feather."

"Oh?" Jane said invitingly.

"I don't much like him. Thomas does."

"Not unreservedly," Thomas put in. "But he is putting some fire and spunk into the tribe."

"And I think 'fire and spunk' just mean discontent," Linda said. "And no, to answer your question, Mrs. Jeffry, HawkHunter's not seriously hurt. But he's refusing to have anything done about replacing his tooth. He's carrying on about that gap in his mouth as if every white man in Colorado had suddenly descended on him at once and pulled out all his teeth with pliers, just because he's an Indian. It's a badge. Proof of prejudice against the whole Indian culture. Blah, blah, blah."

Thomas smiled at her dotingly. "Aw, come on, Linda, it wasn't *that* bad."

"But, Thomas, it was! And it was stupid. Pete Andrews no more represents all whites than you or I represent all Indians. And HawkHunter had no business bothering him a few hours after his uncle was discovered murdered. Anybody would have been upset in that situation and lashed out in some way at a person who annoyed them. It was rude and disrespectful of HawkHunter."

Thomas nodded. "Maybe so. Yeah, you're right about that, but just the same, the tribe's gotten too complacent. Too lazy."

"Too happy?" Linda asked. "Except for some of the guests treating us like tourist attractions and staring at us, tell me how you've ever suffered from being an Indian. We both go to good schools on scholarships and grants we wouldn't have otherwise. We didn't earn them. We got them simply by being Indian."

"Yeah, but haven't you ever seen what happens when our young people go into a store? Security people turn out in droves, just on the assumption that because we're Indians we're going to steal something."

"Thomas, nowadays that happens when any teenager goes into a store."

Having scored this point, she stuck her tongue out at him and grinned.

Thomas looked at Mel and shrugged. "Women," he said. "I'll never be able to outtalk one."

"Oh, Thomas, Thomas, Thomas," Linda groaned. "Can't you hear yourself? You're just as prejudiced as any white. But against a sex instead of a race."

"Linda, it was a *joke!*" Thomas protested.

"So is the tomahawk chop at football games."

"No, that's different. That's—"

"Excuse me!" Jane said. "I didn't mean to start a fight."

"Fight?" Thomas and Linda said in unison, then laughed at each other.

"This isn't a fight," Linda went on. "This is a pleasant chat. We rent the V.F.W. hall and sell tickets when we *really* have a fight. Anyway, there's one thing we do agree on in all this. Little Feather."

"Who is that?" Jane asked. "The woman I saw with HawkHunter in the native costume?"

"Costume is right," Linda said. "She's his wife and she's a bitch."

At this Thomas nodded. "A professional Indian."

Jane smiled. "What does that mean?"

Linda explained. "She's the daughter of a woman who may or may not be one-quarter Indian and a Vietnam vet, also part Indian, who came home and went quietly crazy someplace in the mountains in California. Little Feather, whose real name is something like Sally Jones, grew up one of those malcontents who had to find somebody to blame for everything that was wrong with her life, so she latched onto being an Indian. All that silly feathers-and-beads getup, the medicine woman mystique. She's just a fraud. And I suspect she makes good money on it along the way. That suede outfit wasn't cheap, and she drives a BMW. Even if it's only a rental, it still costs big bucks."

"You know a lot about her," Jane said.

"My cousin Gloria went to school in California with Little Feather's cousin."

A group of customers entered the room and Thomas Whitewing leaped to his feet to go back into waiter mode. "We need to walk off dessert, Jane," Mel said. "We'll see you around, Linda."

As they left the dining room, Mel took Jane's arm and said, "You amaze me. You're the only person I know who can get so completely involved in gossiping about people you don't even know."

"Oh, Mel," she said sorrowfully. "Someday I'll have to explain to you the difference between common gossip and research into the human condition. There's a fine distinction."

"Sure there is," he said.

19

Sunday morning, Jane got up early and prowled around the silent cabin from window to window, watching it snow heavily. She put her boots on and threw a blanket over her nightgown and robe to let Willard out. He didn't enjoy the frigid, blowing snow any more than she did, and they both decided the best plan was to go back to bed. Willard dropped right off, but Jane couldn't get back to sleep. Too many naps, she decided.

Or too many murders on her mind.

After forty-five minutes, she got up again and made herself some hot cocoa. Pulling a chair and an ottoman nearer the glass doors, she settled down with her cocoa and watched the now-diminishing snow. The white cat popped its head up over the railing of the deck. Jane looked around quickly and discovered that Willard hadn't followed her. If he saw the cat and went haywire, he'd wake everybody. The cat sat preening and washing, glancing at Jane every now and then as if for admiration.

"I wonder what you know," Jane said out loud. "If only you could talk."

So much for Shelley's assurances that once they'd organized their thinking, the subconscious could be counted on to sort it all out and supply an answer.

Jane was more confused now than she had been last night. Far from having any glimmer of a solution, she felt mired in unrelated facts, opinions, and information.

Still, she had a weird sense that there was a light on behind a door somewhere in her brain. *In the madman's room.*

She smiled to herself at the recollection. Once, in college, she'd had a rather strange English professor who had assigned as the class's term-paper subject, "Imagination." The students were to come up with a concrete theory that explained imagination, especially in regard to the writers they'd studied that semester. Jane had invented "The Warehouse with the Madman in the Back Room," and hadn't thought about it again for years.

The theory went like this: your brain is a great warehouse where every fact, experience, and sensation is stored. There are acres and acres of shelving. All fairly neatly organized and labeled. At least at first. A child has only a relatively few, but very big, important things stored, and the warehouse manager keeps all that big, important stuff on low shelves near the front where it's easily accessible. The madman— Imagination—can romp around freely, putting a gadget from this fact on that sensation, substituting a gizmo from one bit of information for a thingamabob holding together another two facts. This is why young children are so creative and uninhibited with their imaginations: the madman has free run of the place.

But as time goes on, the warehouse manager, and the outside world, conspire against the madman. The shelves get fuller and fuller. Parents and teachers start requiring the warehouse manager to get his act together and be able to find and supply things more efficiently when they're required. Of necessity, stuff starts getting put on higher shelves, and the warehouse manager can't have the madman capering about recklessly while the manager is climbing ladders to find things.

So the madman gets put away in the back room during the day. He's only free at night, while the manager is sleeping. At night, the madman rules the warehouse, making dreams and nightmares. And sometimes he plays with the shiny new stuff—the nine times tables or the geography of South America. Other stuff he ignores, or actually dislikes enough to destroy—like the seven times tables and the necessity of writing thank-you notes for birthday presents.

And still life goes on. New things keep coming in. The warehouse manager starts running out of easily accessible room, so he begins shoving old stuff farther back on the shelves and putting the new stuff in front. And he's getting older, too. His enthusiasm for doing a perfect job is waning. His organizational skills start slipping. And that damned curious, capering madman is driving him crazy. So eventually he locks the madman up entirely. Only on rare occasions does the manager forget to lock up the madman's room at night, and he gets out and bats around, creating wild dreams.

In Jane's theory, a writer could make use of the madman, but not with any reliability. When the writer needed something, the warehouse manager would tear up one aisle and down another, tossing random bits of this and that, old movies, new sensations, mislabeled facts, dusty old memories into a basket, which he'd then toss in the back room to the mad-man. The madman, thrilled with these toys, would re-assemble the bits into something barely recognizable and toss it back out for the writer to use. It was all supplies from the writer's own mental warehouse, but in a form nobody had ever imagined before.

Jane hadn't thought about the madman for a long time, but now she sensed that the light was on in his little cell at the back of the warehouse. She'd been here for only two full days, but she'd dumped a lot of new material on the doorstep of the warehouse and she had the belief—or was it only the longing to believe?—that she knew nearly everything she needed to know to make sense of the seemingly senseless deaths. If only the warehouse manager would toss the right facts, impressions, and sensa-tions to the madman. Maybe she could figure out why Bill Smith and Doris Schmidtheiser had been killed. Then she could close off the "Colorado Vaca-tion" shelf and get on with her life without having to keep on wondering.

But forty-eight hours from now she'd be on her way home—provided the sheriff didn't detain her! No, she couldn't even contemplate that. Even getting away from here was going to be awful. They had an eight o'clock flight, which meant that they'd all have to be up and moving pretty briskly by five at the lat-est to get everything, including Willard, packed up, down the mountain, through rush-hour Denver traffic, and to the airport. They'd have to return the rental car, check Willard and the baggage through, and all without losing any of the kids. Ugh! What a thought. It might just be easier to stay up very, very late and

never go to bed at all Monday night. If only there
were an airport closer.

She stared out the window at Flattop.

Airport. . . ?

Airport!

She leaped up and ran to the bedroom. Shaking
Shelley's arm, she said, "Wake up, Shelley. I've got
to talk to you. I've got an idea!"

"What time is it?" Shelley asked her pillow.

"Time? Oh, time. Almost nine, I think."

"Fix. . . coffee. . ." Shelley mumbled.

"Okay, but hurry and wake up."

She started the coffeemaker and ran back to the
bedroom to check on Shelley's progress. Her bed was
empty and the shower was running. Good.

Jane paced around excitedly until the coffee was
ready and Shelley emerged. "Now, what is this?"
Shelley demanded as Jane handed her a steaming
cup.

"Come to the window. Look at the hill."

"Uh-huh. It's still there."

"Describe it."

"A little mountain with the top cut off," Shelley
said.

"But it's long and flat. It isn't a mountain, it's a
long, straight ridge with the top cut off. Now, do you
remember the last thing I said up there before we
skied down?"

"Something about breaking your neck and me rais-
ing your children?"

"No. You were saying it was a long, flat place
where you might expect to find a cemetery, and I said
you could land a 747 up there."

Shelley turned from contemplating the mountain to stare at Jane. "An airport," she said quietly.

"Yes. An airport. Think how good for business an airport up here would be."

Shelley sat down on one of the sofas. "Let me think."

"Don't you see how much more valuable an airport would make this place?" Jane said. "And HawkHunter wants the Indians to own that land. From what Tenny said, he was making threats to try to take the whole resort, but I'll bet that was just a ploy to get Bill, or the new owners, to settle and get rid of him by giving the tribe the hill. Just that little old useless, bunny-slope hill. With the cemetery at the top that Linda Moosefoot had never heard of, even though she's part of the tribe."

Shelley shook her head as if to clear it. "Okay. Okay. Say HawkHunter had this airport idea and was trying to force somebody to give up the land to the tribe so they could build an airport and make a—forgive the term—killing. Are you casting him as Bill's murderer because of it?"

Jane stopped pacing and flung herself onto the other sofa. "I was, but I'm not sure why." She thought for a minute. "Okay. Here's one way: HawkHunter wants to get this land from Bill and thinks Bill's more likely to cave in than the investors—"

"Logical so far."

"But when Bill gets Paul up here, and Bill is apparently going through with the sale, HawkHunter stages the protest to make things difficult. Bill is mad at HawkHunter for queering the deal and tells HawkHunter if he doesn't lay off, Bill will just keep the damned place and build the airport himself on the top of the ridge. The tribe knows Bill is a man of few words, but he really means the few words he says. HawkHunter sees his cause is lost now. But if he kills Bill, he accomplishes two things. He really scares the investors off, which is what it looks like has happened with Paul clearing out, *and* he doesn't have to worry about Bill's threat to build the airport. He knows from the tribe that Joanna wouldn't take on a big, new project like that. She'd be hard pressed just to keep the place going on an even keel. Besides, Joanna is much more likely to cave in to HawkHunter's demands than Bill ever was."

She sat back, looking smug.

"What about Doris?" Shelley asked.

Jane stopped looking smug. "I don't know. Hell. Maybe she overheard them talking about it?"

Shelley shook her head. "And if killing Bill was a deliberate attempt to scare off the investors, why dress the snowman up like a king and make it look like it had to do with the genealogists?"

"Okay. Good points," Jane said sadly.

"Cheer up," Shelley said. "We may be on the right track with this airport thing and just be looking at it wrong. What would you think about just talking to Tenny about the idea of an airport here—without voicing any suspicions of anyone—and seeing what she says?"

"I think it's a good idea. We might learn something valuable."

Shelley gave Tenny a call and said she'd like to talk to her about something. Tenny seemed glad to hear from her and said she was on her way to the resort office to do a little paperwork. They could just ask for her at the desk there whenever they wanted.

Jane and Shelley dressed hurriedly and woke Katie to say they were leaving for a bit and not to let anyone in while they were gone. Then they set out to trudge to the lodge. The heavy snow was now only a blowing mist off the pines, and everything looked incredibly clean and crisp. "It's hard to believe there's mud and pine cones and trash under all this, isn't it?" Jane said.

Halfway down the road, they had to climb onto the snowbank at the side to let a snowplow grumble by. As they stood there, Shelley said, "Don't look right now, but there's somebody following us."

Jane's heart gave a frantic lurch, but she pretended to gaze around casually and spotted a man in a navy ski outfit lurking farther up the road. "I think I recognize him," she said quietly. "One of the sheriff's men."

"I wonder if he's protecting us or spying on us," Shelley said.

"I don't think I like either choice."

When they got to the lodge, the receptionist said that Tenny was, indeed, in her office, but was on the phone now if they wanted to wait.

"Let's go to the gift shop," Shelley suggested.

"I can't afford to go in there again," Jane said. "I'll wait out front. I want to see what's become of our 'escort.' "

"Get a load of the bulletin board," Shelley said.

A listing of events on a large board in the lobby was constantly being updated. This morning it announced that HawkHunter would be doing a reading from his best-selling book, *I, HawkHunter,* in Lounge

A at 7:00 P.M. on Monday night. Public invited. Reception to follow. Cost: $5, to be donated to the Native American Legal Rights Fund.

"I don't know if it's admirably open-minded or just plain stupid of the Smiths to offer him a forum," Shelley muttered. She went off shaking her head in wonder.

Someone had just shoveled the front walk and the sun had emerged for a moment. The light hitting the brickwork made it steam. Jane sat down on one of the benches and looked around. There was no sign of the navy-clad officer. Maybe he'd come into the lodge behind them and was watching her from inside. Or maybe he was trailing after Shelley.

Jane gazed at the bricks at her feet. She hadn't noticed before, but they were laid in a very unusual herringbone pattern. She'd been thinking about bricking over her cement patio in the spring, and this would be a nice pattern to copy. At first, as she studied the design to memorize it, she wasn't consciously aware of the oddly shaped, shiny white pebble next to her foot. Then she picked it up idly to toss away and realized it wasn't a pebble.

It was a tooth! Of all the weird things to find. But of course! It must be HawkHunter's tooth. The one Pete had knocked out in their fight right here. She couldn't quite bring herself to throw it away. When HawkHunter got over being so proud of missing it, he'd probably want to get the hole in his mouth filled in, and the original tooth might serve as the best model for a replacement. She'd give it to Linda Moosefoot to give back to him, she thought, slipping it into her pocket.

"Jane, I've discovered the mother lode of the best

cinnamon rolls in the world," Shelley said from behind her. "I'm going to hate going home to my own cooking."

Tenny joined them in the casual dining room just as they were being seated. When the waiter had brought their coffee and taken orders, Shelley said, "Tenny, we were wondering about Flattop. Had your uncle ever thought of using it for an airport runway?"

"Of course," Tenny said. "He talked about it for years, but he had some geologists out three years ago, and it's impossible. Shelley, what's wrong? You look as disappointed as Uncle Bill was."

20

"It has to do with the quality and type of the rock," Tenny went on. "The central core of the ridge is very hard, but too narrow for a runway. At least a runway that would take a big plane. You could land puddle jumpers up there, but not anything really commercial. Everything to the sides is—I can't remember the name they called it—something too soft and crumbly anyway. Uncle Bill had two different groups of geologists in and they both agreed that you'd have to virtually shore up the entire ridge along the length to take the impact of a heavy plane landing. That's all in the report Uncle Bill prepared for your husband. Why do you ask?"

"No reason," Shelley said. "It just crossed our minds that it might be an option." She glared at Jane as if it were all her fault.

"Is there any word about your uncle?" Jane asked, hurriedly changing the subject.

"From the sheriff? No, I'm afraid not. He says he's 'pursuing several leads,' but won't say what they are."

I hope having that silly deputy follow me around constitutes pursuing a lead, Jane thought grumpily.

"I brought something along that might interest you," Tenny said, reaching for an accordian-file folder she'd been carrying and had laid aside when they first sat down. Extracting a five-by-seven white envelope, she removed from it an old picture—a posed professional photograph mounted in a fancy brown cardstock designed to fold out and stand up. "Aunt Joanna and I found this with some of Uncle Bill's things. It must be the one photograph I told you he once mentioned."

The picture was of a couple and two young children. The boy, presumably Bill Smith, was about three and wearing a "farmer's boy" outfit, little overalls with a plaid shirt, but these weren't clothes just for a picture. A barely discernible patch on one knee attested to the fact that these were the best of his everyday clothes. The little girl, Pete Andrews's mother, was about two years old and wearing a very simple, unfrilly little dress that likewise was probably the best of everyday. She had a blond Buster Brown hairdo, ornamented with a big bow that matched her dress.

The mother was a thin, tired-looking woman. She must have died not very long after this picture was taken, and there was a hint of illness already in the drawn lines of her pretty face. Although the picture must have been taken in the early 1930s, the age of bobbed hair, the woman either hadn't known the fashion or hadn't chosen to follow it. Her hair, dark blond and curly, was pulled into a thick knot at the back of her neck. Wispy tendrils had escaped around her face. She wore a severe dress of a light, print pattern with only a narrow white collar and matching belt as decoration. This was clearly a farm wife, but oddly enough, with her plain garb and hair, she wore what looked very much like diamond earrings and a rather elaborate, sparkling necklace. She also wore two rings on the hand that came around the toddler on her lap. Her other hand, behind the little boy and probably hanging onto him as he stood on the photographer's plush little bench beside her, wasn't visible.

"Look at the jewelry," Jane said softly to Shelley as they both studied the photograph.

"It was in an old-fashioned wooden cigar box with the picture," Tenny said, also lowering her voice. "The necklace, earrings, and three rings. I'm putting them in a safe-deposit box first thing in the morning."

"Did you and your aunt know about this jewelry?"

"I didn't, but she did. Uncle Bill tried to give it to her when they were first married, but she said it wasn't her style and he'd better save it for when they had a daughter. Of course, they never did, and she said after a while she forgot about it and didn't remember until we found it. She's given it to me." Tenny started to tear up as she spoke and took a quick gulp of her coffee.

Jane turned her attention to the man in the picture. The first thing one noticed about him was the difference in the colors of his face. He was obviously a man who was normally bearded and hatted and out in the sun, but he shaved the beard and put aside the hat for the photograph. His upper cheeks, nose, and the lower half of his forehead were a good three shades darker than the rest of his clean-shaven face. His hair, long and shaggy, had been slicked back, leaving his face looking vulnerable and oddly naked.

Yet it was a rather startling face. Handsome in a fierce way, with thick brows, an imposing jaw, and the kind of large, somewhat close, almost transparently blue eyes often seen in Civil War-era photographs. It was obvious from that lean, strong, almost angry face that having a picture taken wasn't his free choice. He wore a black suit that must have been old-fashioned even during those days, and a suspiciously stiff white collar that bit into his strong, thick neck. It must have been purchased specifically for the photo and was probably never worn again. In fact, Jane could imagine him ripping it off and flinging it away as soon as the photographer snapped the shot.

And yet, for all his fierceness, he rested one hand gently on his wife's arm. It was a tender gesture—protective, supportive—and obviously spontaneous rather than posed. Perhaps he suspected that she would not grow old with him. Maybe that was why a man who wouldn't permit a photograph of himself had shaved and put on his good suit—probably his only suit—and posed for this. Not to have a picture of himself, but to have one of her before it was too late.

The studio name printed on the cardboard surround was located in Denver. So this thin, frail, doomed wife must have persuaded him to have the picture taken (perhaps not so very much against his will), not locally, but in the city where no one would know them. In those days, before I-70 and the Eisenhower Tunnel, the trip must have been a long, arduous one. Jane tried to imagine driving up over the Continental Divide in a 1920s vintage automobile and shuddered. Maybe there'd been a train instead.

"Jane?" Shelley elbowed her.

"I'm sorry. My imagination was running away,"

Jane answered. "Tenny, are you sure this is Bill and his family?"

"Yes. There is another picture, a wedding picture, of this woman that is labeled. It's clearly the same person. And there are several other pictures of Uncle Bill as a child, and they are the same child as this little boy."

"But this isn't labeled?" Jane asked, turning it over.

"No. We slid it out of the folder to look, and there's no writing on the back."

"Your uncle certainly took more after his mother than his father," Shelley said.

"And he doesn't look Rasputin-ish in this picture," Jane said. "In fact, he's quite good-looking."

They chatted for a while about the details of the pictures; then Tenny carefully put the photograph back into the envelope. "I'm glad we found this and I appreciate having someone to show it to, but I'd be very grateful if you didn't tell anyone from the Holnagrad Society about it," she said. "I understand their enthusiasm and interest, but I don't want them harassing Aunt Joanna just now."

"Tenny, we wouldn't mention it to anyone, even if you hadn't asked," Jane assured her.

"Thanks, Jane. Now I've got to get going."

"Tenny, just one question before you run off," Shelley said. "I noticed the announcement in the lobby about HawkHunter doing a reading Monday."

"Yes," Tenny said grimly. "Another clever arrangement of Pete's. Before he and HawkHunter fell out. I'd love to find a way to cancel that, but HawkHunter is so damned litigious, I don't dare."

"Has Pete turned up?" Shelley asked.

"Oh, yes. About eight this morning. Hung over. Apologetic. Inclined to weep," she said contemptuously.

Shelley watched Tenny as she threaded her way through the tables and out of the dining room. "What are you thinking?" Jane asked her.

"Bad thoughts," Shelley said. "Very bad thoughts." She glanced around, making sure nobody else was close enough to overhear them. "You know, we've been trying to figure out how Pete, for example, could be the murderer. Mainly because we don't much like him and because he's pretty much of a moral weakling. But we don't know that, really. We know only what Tenny has told us about him. And we believe it because Tenny says so and we like her. She's *us,* if you know what I mean. She's a fortyish woman, speaks our language, and appears to be quite forthright."

"Agreed," Jane said, suspecting she knew what was coming next.

"But murderers can, in theory, be quite pleasant, normal-seeming people. You're always hearing people say, when someone's arrested for murder, 'We never suspected! He seemed so normal!' So—"

"So maybe we've been taken in by Tenny? I'd hate to think that."

"So would I, but it's possible, Jane. And she's certainly involved in everything here and might be a good deal more involved than we suspect."

Jane nodded reluctantly. "I bet the same thing triggered this in you as it did in me. The mention of that jewelry."

"Exactly. It's hard to tell in a black-and-white photo, but it looked to me like the jewelry Bill's mother was wearing was worth a king's ransom. It really could have been some of Russia's—or Holnagrad's—crown jewels."

"It probably was real. The way the woman was dressed, it was clear that she didn't care about what my grandmother would have called 'fripperies.' She obviously had very simple taste. And yet she was wearing jewelry that was completely inappropriate to her clothing, not to mention to the frontierish way she must have lived. So the jewelry was out of keeping and very probably worn because her husband believed that if you had those jewels, you wore them in pictures. I loved that picture, by the way. It made me feel I knew those people. I found myself imagining that I knew them very, very well, in fact."

"I could tell you were taken with it," Shelley said affectionately. "The way you got that goofy, faraway look. Anyhow, my thinking was this: if I were a murderer—"

Jane snorted.

"No, listen. If I were a murderer, or somebody with anything important to hide, I would try to be as open and honest as possible. People are naturally suspicious of anyone who's secretive and guilty-acting or unpleasant. If you ask someone a seemingly innocent question and they answer by saying it's none of your damned business, or by being excessively sly about not answering, your first thought is that they're hiding something, right?"

"Or that it really is none of my business and I was damned rude for asking," Jane said. "Sorry. No jokes. Yes, I agree. If I were trying to hide something, I'd give as much of the truth as I could, and hope that the parts I left out weren't very noticeable."

"Exactly. So what might her seeming openness be hiding? To be blunt, she came out of Bill Smith's death with what might well be a fortune in jewelry."

"—and cotrusteeship of a huge estate—"

"—And possible proof of a valuable genealogical connection to the Tsars of Russia."

"Not proof of *her* connection," Jane pointed out.

"But proof that might be valuable to someone else. Proof that might be either provided or withheld. For a price. She asked us not to mention that picture to anyone, remember? That could be innocent. Just a natural desire for privacy. Or it could be because she wants to spring the picture on someone else at the optimum moment."

Jane stirred the dregs of her coffee. "She's benefited enormously from his death, hasn't she?"

Shelley nodded. "I'm afraid so. More so than anybody else except her aunt. Certainly more than Pete, who'd make a much better villain. But what would the connection to Doris be?"

"The Tsar thing in some way. Suppose Doris was so humiliated by the debate that she decided to give it up and throw in the towel?"

"Can you really imagine her doing that?"

"No," Jane said, "but I can imagine her saying so in the first moments of stress and embarrassment. A sort of flounce. Meant to make somebody pet her and fuss over her and talk her out of it. But if she said it too forcefully to the wrong person, she might have been accidentally taken seriously."

"The great problem with all of this," Shelley said, "is that Tenny knew better than anyone how little time Bill had to live. She knew all she had to do was wait a while."

"We only have her word about that," Jane said.

"No, we have Linda Moosefoot's, too. Remember, Linda told you she knew because Tenny had had Linda drive her to a Denver hospital."

"That's right. I'd forgotten. But that still doesn't mean something could have precipitated things. I mean, suppose Doris had said she was giving it up, or something else that caused Tenny to kill her. If Bill found out, or even suspected, he might have told her he was going to change the trust. Make Pete the co-trustee. Leave her out in the cold. Maybe specify in the trust that the jewels were to go to Pete. They really should have, if you look at it from the viewpoint of relationships. Tenny is no relation to Bill Smith at all. Pete is actually his nephew—born into the bloodline that originally owned the jewels. They should have belonged jointly to Bill and his sister. When Bill had no children, they should have gone to his sister's child."

"Well, that's one way of looking at it," Shelley said. "But he probably considered that they were his wife's to do with as she wanted."

"She obviously felt that way."

"I don't like this," Shelley said.

"Neither do I. It's not pleasant to see a bunch of facts lining up against our instinct and judgment."

"Nor should we be talking about it here," Shelley said. A group of guests had taken a table near them. Near enough to overhear. "Let's go back to the cabin. Maybe the walk in the cold air will clear our brains."

"There speaks desperation," Jane said. "But anything's possible."

Shelley, Jane, and Mel decided the best way to spend the rest of their Sunday in the mountains was anywhere but at the resort. The kids didn't agree, but hadn't any good alternative to suggest, so were forced to go along on an extended drive. Shelley and Paul had rented a huge, luxurious van and Paul had left it for their use. But Jane wouldn't think of letting Shelley drive.

"She's my dearest friend in the world, Mel," Jane said, "but when she gets her hands on a steering wheel, she turns into a maniac. Something viciously competitive goes on in her brain and she turns into the Hitler of the Highway. Wants to own the whole of it from curb to curb. Please, if you value your sanity, don't let her drive!"

When they all had assembled in the parking lot, Mel said, "Shelley, this is your vacation and you ought to get to relax and look at the scenery. Let me do the driving, why don't you?"

Shelley looked at him. Then at Jane. "You've been talking about me behind my back, Jane."

"Not really. I didn't say anything to Mel I haven't said to you about your driving."

"I'll bet you told him about that Army convoy."

"Not a word," Jane said, shivering at the recollection.

"If a bunch of soldiers can't cope with being passed on a tiny little hill—which I could see beyond perfectly well—without going to pieces and running up on the shoulder, I'd like to know what sort of help they'd be in a war!" Shelley said indignantly.

Mel drove.

And they had a lovely day. They went back to I-70 and east to the turnoff to Golden. The scenery along the narrow mountain roads was breathtaking, and when they emerged onto a stretch of high plains, it was even more so. The world had never looked so vast, clean, and beautiful. Jane and Shelley firmly squashed Mike's proposal that nobody should visit Golden without tasting a pitcher of Coors at its birthplace. They went on to Boulder, the quintessential red-roofed college town in the foothills, and Mike looked it over with the greedy eyes of a high school senior. Jane saw it through the eyes of a parent who might have to pay the out-of-state tuition and blanched.

From Boulder they took a back road that led to a town called Nederland, where Shelley claimed there was a magnificent rock-and-jewelry shop. She was right, of course, and once again Jane was left to marvel at her friend's uncanny ability to home in on superb shopping opportunities. Halfway across a continent, on unfamiliar ground, Shelley had managed to know, as if by instinct, about this small shop in a tiny town high in the mountains. It was amazing.

Jane admired a necklace of polished red agate beads, which Mel insisted on buying for her. Jane put

up only token resistance to his generosity. The necklace would look magnificent with her new outfit.

They made it from Nederland to Estes Park, where
they ate and spent several hours driving on some of
the roads that were kept cleared in the winter. Finally
it was three o'clock, and fearing a sudden sunset,
which is how sunsets happen in the mountains, they
headed back to the resort.

Jane had discovered that her children, freed from
their late father's dictatorial concept of vacationing,
made pretty good travelers, and she spent much of
the return trip in quiet consideration of taking a family trip when school was out. Where to go? A resort
in Wisconsin, perhaps? No, a trip to Williamsburg.
She had been there as a child and loved it. There
would be lots of things to interest all of them in
Williamsburg. Of course, she'd have to let Mike do
part of the driving. That thought brought her to the
next, which was about vehicles. Her poor old station
wagon would hardly make it beyond the suburbs of
Chicago. There were days when she wondered if the
station wagon was going to make it past the pothole
at the end of the driveway.

"What are you scowling about?" Mel asked glancing at her in the rearview mirror.

"Cars," she answered. "Cars and money. Are we
almost there? I'm hungry again."

Mel had been driving and Shelley had taken over
the other front seat as dictator/guide. Every time
they'd piled out and back into the van, Jane had
ended up farther back. Now she was in the rearmost
seat by herself. As they once again headed across the
high plains outside Golden, there was surprisingly little traffic, and Jane's imagination kicked into gear.

Looking out to the right, she could see nothing but mile after gently undulating mile of snow, ringed by rugged mountains. The setting sun caused the mountains to cast long blue shadows, and here and there were simple wooden structures, hunkering down against the wind and the drifting snow. A half-remembered scene from a movie, probably *Doctor Zhivago,* superimposed itself on the landscape, and Jane found herself thinking it might not be so strange after all to find an exiled Russian here.

Had old Gregory actually been who Doris thought he was? And if so, why had he come here? How could he have known about this desolately beautiful place? And why would it have appealed to him? She smiled at the recollection of a conversation she'd overheard between two of the genealogists at a nearby table the day before. One had been talking about one of his ancestors coming from Sweden and settling in northern Minnesota. "Most of our ancestors came to this country," he'd said, "and wandered around until they found some place just as shitty as the place they'd left."

Had Gregory craved the hostile solitude of the Russian steppes? Had he somehow needed the bitter cold and blowing snow? Or had Gregory Smith just been a man named Gregory Smith and nothing else, who had meant to go to California and only got this far before giving up the trek? Maybe he'd been making his way through the mountains, stopped on a pleasant day to do a little gold panning or to explore an interesting crevasse, and found riches. That was certainly possible.

But if that were the case, where and how had he come by the jewels he later gave his wife? Had he found enough gold to buy them? Who could say? His life before his marriage was a mystery. He might have had his eye on the pretty local girl and taken the train to Chicago or New York to buy the jewelry as a wedding gift. Jane wondered if there were actually any Holnagrad crown jewels that history had recorded. It would take a team of experts to make the connection, if so. And Doris had been just that kind of expert. Was it even remotely possible that Doris had known about the jewels, or suspected their existence? And if she had, would she have kept quiet about it? Probably not, but Jane had to admit that she wasn't in a good position to speculate about Doris. She had hardly known the woman. They'd had one brief conversation and then a collision in a hallway.

All she knew about Doris was either surface impressions or from what other people said. Mainly what Lucky Lucke had said about her. Was there any reason to doubt his interpretation of her character? Jane simply couldn't guess. She didn't know anything more about him than she'd known about Doris.

At the exit where they turned off I-70 for the final leg of the drive, Mel stopped for gas. They all got out to stretch their legs. Shelley approached Jane. "Are you feeling like I am? The thought of returning to the resort and having to keep an eagle eye on the kids is oppressive."

Jane nodded. "I didn't quite realize what it was until you put it in words, but I'm not anxious to get back, either. Except that I have to let Willard out for a run. It's a lovely place, but given the circumstances . . ."

"Then let's just stay long enough to tend to Willard and change our clothes, and then go out somewhere away from the resort for dinner. It'll be my treat. Someplace elegant?"

"I like the part about your treat, but I've had my quota of elegance," Jane said. "How about someplace really inelegant? Barbecue, maybe? Burger King would be even better."

Everybody else agreed, but Jane was outvoted on Willard. "Either he's destroyed the place by now or he hasn't. Another half hour isn't going to matter," was Mel's opinion, and the others agreed.

"Besides," Shelley put in, "Linda Moosefoot has been around to clean, most likely, and she probably let him out, seeing as we were all gone."

There was a Burger King diagonally across the interchange. They considerately let the kids go in first so they wouldn't have to be seen traveling with adults; then Jane, Shelley, and Mel wandered in a moment later and took places at the opposite side of the room.

"You're very quiet today," Mel said while he and Jane waited for Shelley to bring their food.

"I was thinking about Russia and old Gregory Smith and a lot of things. And, I have to admit, I'm a little bit homesick—and I'm enjoying it."

"You're liking being homesick?" Mel asked.

"Yes. See, the whole time I was growing up, we had no home. With my father being in the diplomatic corps, we were always moving. I never went to the same school for two years. Sometimes I didn't even manage two semesters in the same place. And we didn't really even have a home base. We lived in some pretty fancy surroundings every now and then, but they were never ours to keep and come back to. So when we bought the house I live in, back when

Mike was a baby, I was determined I wouldn't leave until I was taken out on a gurney. And it's neat to discover that I really have become so attached to one place that I miss it."

Mel took her hand and just smiled at her.

"On the other hand," she went on, "homesick or not, I'm not real sure the sheriff is going to be willing for me to leave, and even when I do, it'll drive me wild not ever knowing what happened here. Sure you feel that, too, Mel."

He opened his mouth to deny the charge, but stopped and reluctantly shook his head. "I'm on vacation, I keep telling myself. But I still hate to see an investigation of a murder—very possibly two murders—going nowhere. But I don't have access to any inside information. For all I know, they're working round the clock on fiber analysis, DNA testing, fingerprinting, and who knows what. But without knowing any of the results, I can't see how I can form any opinions."

Shelley had arrived and was distributing their food and drinks while he said this. "But, Mel, all that has to do with *after* the crime," she said.

He looked at her blankly. "Of course it does. Why would anybody bother with it before a crime is committed?"

"No, what Shelley means is that the crime itself has something to do with relationships. Not with science. The relationships and the emotions they provoke are the cause, and if you can figure out the cause, then the science part can fill in the rest."

Mel nodded. "So what do you see as the cause?"

"That's the problem," Jane said. "I don't know. There are so many possibilities. The potential sale of the resort is certainly one element that might have provoked the crime, or crimes. There's nothing like money to get people's emotions to a fever pitch. And the genealogy thing, the claim that Bill Smith was the rightful Tsar, has endless possibilities of emotional involvement. Money again. Glory. Power. Jealousy. For that matter, the motivation could, in some complex way, be related to both the sale and the claim to the tsardom—if that's a word."

Mel had been unwrapping his burger and removing anything that resembled a vegetable. "So if you don't have a suggestion, aren't we right back to science and not having access?"

Shelley, salting her fries, joined in. "We should be, but I have a feeling we know the solution and just don't know we know."

Mel rolled his eyes, but Jane agreed. "I think so, too, Shelley. I keep having the sense that if we'd just put the right facts and impressions into the correct order, the answer would be obvious. I still haven't given Lucky the file folder that Doris dropped. Maybe when I do, he'll let me look at some of her other documents. Maybe there's something there that will make things fall together."

"But, Jane, we don't know enough about genealogy to make any sense of her notes anyway. What we need could be in them, but it's like reading a foreign language. One of those courses they were giving was about how to construct a tiny tafel."

"What's that?" Mel asked.

Shelley shrugged. "I have no idea, except that it's a list of some kind. I just remembered it because it was such a weird phrase. That's the point. If the motive does have to do with genealogy, you and I don't know where or how to look, and we wouldn't recognize it if it walked up to us with a tag around its neck."

Mel was shaking his head while he chewed. The women waited patiently for him to swallow.

"In my experience," he finally said, "murder usually has to do with money or passion. High passion. Not things like power or prestige. Those are pretty pale emotions compared to passion. Now, most of these people, including the two victims, were, to put it politely, 'mature' individuals. Most people of that age have their passions well under control. If they didn't, they'd be in jail or a mental institution. Can you really imagine Mrs. Schmidtheiser and Bill Smith having a wild sexual affair? If so, you can cast Mrs. Smith in the role of suspect."

"Mel!" Jane said, scandalized.

"The other kind of passion is all sorts of things that fall under the heading of self-defense," he went on, ignoring her. "Defense in physical terms, of course, but often defense of a lifework. Let's say you—wait, let me think of a good one. Okay, suppose you'd won an Olympic gold medal in something like speed skating, and in forty years your record still hadn't been broken. You've spent those forty years teaching, pontificating, being a celebrity on the strength of it. Every four years when the Olympics roll around, the newspeople come and do nice, flattering film pieces on you. Then one day someone comes up to you and says he has proof that you had tiny little rockets attached to your skates when you won."

Jane smiled at the image.

"It's silly, but don't you see? You've made that

record your lifework. Your entire reputation rests on a cheat and here's somebody threatening your life, in a sense."

Jane nodded. "Like Bill's resort, which was his lifework, and Doris's research, which was hers."

"But, Jane, the difference is, I'm talking about perpetrators—and they were the victims," Mel said.

There was a moment's thick silence before Jane said, "Hell! So what's the point?"

"Don't get defensive," he said. "I'm just pointing out the reasons I think it has to come back to money. It's the only thing that makes sense and provides a strong enough motive."

"And the only large amounts of money at stake here involve the resort," Shelley said.

"If that's true, how does Doris figure in?" Jane asked. "It's not as if she'd stand to profit if the resort was sold or wasn't."

"Unless she knew something that would prevent the sale," Shelley said. "If either Pete or Tenny really thought they would profit from the sale and Doris knew—oh, maybe that Bill wasn't really Gregory's son and thus didn't really own the land—wouldn't that make it worthwhile to stop her from telling anyone?"

"Jeez! That's a bizarre thought," Jane said. "Everybody's been concentrating on who Gregory really was, but nobody's questioned who Bill really was. And Doris had spent years snooping around the family relationships."

"I'm afraid I was just giving an example, Jane," Shelley said. "And a bad one at that. You're forgetting about that old photograph."

"Not entirely. That little boy looked a lot like the

mother in the picture, but he was just a cute little boy who could have grown up to look like anybody. He might not have been the older man we knew as Bill Smith. Remember, Tenny told us that the mother died when Bill was very little, and Gregory pretty much left it to some of the tribal women to take care of him. Suppose, for some weird reason, one of them had substituted another child—"

And even as Jane was speaking, she heard how stupid it sounded.

"I'm sorry," she said. "My brain's run amok."

"I'm so glad you were the one to say that," Mel muttered. "Everybody done? Let's get back to see what that fleabag dog of yours has done."

After they'd gotten back on the road and were nearing the resort, Shelley said, "Jane, I think I've got a blister on my heel. I want to run in the gift shop and get a bandage for it. Will you come along and walk back with me?"

"I'll come with you, too," Mike said. "There's something I need."

Mel took the rest of the kids back to the cabins and Jane sat in the lobby, waiting for Shelley and Mike to return. As she waited, Lucky passed through with an armload of notebooks and file folders. When he saw her sitting alone, he came and sat down. "Are you teaching a class?" she asked.

"No, just finished one. The last of the evening."

"Oh! I'm glad I ran into you," Jane said. She'd reached into her jacket pocket for a tissue and had felt something else. She pulled out the tooth. "I've been meaning to give you this. It's HawkHunter's tooth. I found it out by the front door. The snow had melted back there and it appeared. If you think it might help in making a mold or something for a bridge, you can give it to him."

Lucky took the tooth, glanced at it, and handed it back. "Sorry, but that's not HawkHunter's tooth."

Jane laughed. "How many people have lost teeth by the front door?"

"I don't know, but this is someone else's," Lucky said.

"How do you know?"

"It's easy," he said. And he showed her.

—— 22 ——

When they got back to the condo, they found Linda chatting with the girls. "Hi, Mrs. Jeffry, Mrs. Nowack," she said, heading for her jacket. "I stopped in to check that everything was all right here. The sheriff called Tenny and said he couldn't find any of you."

"What did he want us for?" Jane asked.

"Nothing in particular," Linda said. "At least I don't think so. Just wondered where everybody had gone. Don't worry, I'll call him back for you. Unless you want to talk to him?"

"God forbid!" Jane exclaimed. "Has Willard wrecked anything?"

"Willard?" Linda got a mushy expression. "He wouldn't do a thing like that. Oh, the Sunday papers were all over the living room and there was an awful lot of dog spit on the sliding glass doors—"

"That cat's been back, I'd guess," Jane said.

"I took him out for a while and he chased some squirrels," Linda said. "That made him happy. I'm going home. It's been a long day. Is there anything else you need before I leave?"

"Nothing. Thanks. Oh—there is one thing," Jane said.

"What's that?"

"I know you're going to think I've lost the last of my marbles, but—well—as dumb as it sounds, could I look at the back of your teeth?"

Linda burst out laughing. "Do you think you can fit your head in my mouth to do that?"

Jane was blushing with embarrassment, which made her feel all the sillier. "No, I just want to stick my compact mirror behind your front teeth."

Linda nodded. "Oh, I get it."

"I don't!" Shelley exclaimed. "Have you both gone nuts?"

Jane fished her compact out of her purse and slipped the edge of the mirror behind Linda's upper teeth. Linda was grinning around the mirror. "Shelley, look at the back of Linda's front teeth—"

"Okay," Shelley said suspiciously.

"Now, get another mirror and look at the back of mine."

Shelley did as she was told. Her eyes widened and she looked at each of them again. "Wow!"

Linda removed the mirror. "Shovel incisors, it's called. Indians' front teeth cup on the back side. I think Orientals' teeth do, too, but Occidentals are much flatter."

"That's so strange!" Shelley said.

"There are skull differences, too, but I don't know what they are," Linda said, pulling on her outdoor boots.

"Jane, how did you know about this?" Shelley asked.

"I ran into Lucky and told him I'd found HawkHunter's tooth in the snow. He just glanced at it and said it couldn't be HawkHunter's because of this shovel-incisor thing."

"How weird," Shelley said. "How many people do you think have lost a tooth by the front door lately?"

Jane shrugged. "I don't know. I guess it might even be an animal's tooth. I didn't ask him that."

"Well, if you think I'm letting you stick my compact in Willard's mouth—!" Shelley said, horrified.

"I'm sure Willard wouldn't mind," Linda said. There was a knock on the door. "That's Thomas come to walk me home. See you ladies later."

They thanked her effusively for her attentions and Jane stood at the door, waving her off. Thomas Whitewing had an arm around her as they slogged off through the darkness. When Jane came back in, Shelley had poured each of them a glass of white wine.

"You were very quiet on the way back here," Shelley said. "Were you thinking about that weird tooth thing?"

"No, actually I was thinking about immigrants. Or, I guess they're emigrants when they move within their own country. You and I were struggling and gasping as we came up the hill through the snow, but think of the thousands of women who literally walked over this mountain without the benefit of fancy waterproof snow boots and down-filled nylon parkas."

"Funny, I'd thought about that, too, as we were driving back here this afternoon," Shelley said. "But I was thinking that many of them either set out pregnant or became pregnant along the way. Some even had babies just before or during the trek."

Jane got up and prodded at the fire Mel had started before taking the boys back to his place. "I was talking to Mel about being homesick. I guess that's what started me thinking about it. We can go anywhere in the world now and not be too far from contact with those we left behind. Even if you're a missionary in the Andes, you can still walk down the mountain to a town and send a fax or make a long-distance call. But when all those immigrants came here, they were really leaving behind everything and everybody they knew. If you left some little village along the Rhine to move to St. Louis or some place, you could pretty well count on never seeing the people at home again. Your parents, maybe. Brothers and sisters. You could write—if you knew how—but letters could take months to get back and forth, if they made it at all. You'd leave knowing you wouldn't be able to go to your mother's funeral or ever see your sister's next baby—"

Shelley shook her head. "Not necessarily. That's one of the things the teacher talked about in that beginner's class I took the other day. It's something called chain migration. A town would sometimes collect the money to send some representatives of a couple of families to America to find a suitable place to move to. Then, once the place was chosen, they would follow along in a chain. The young bachelors first, to buy land and build a few houses, then some young families, and eventually the older generation. Sometimes, the teacher said, virtually the entire town moved itself halfway around the globe."

Jane smiled. "That's interesting. And it makes me feel better about it. I'm going to have to call my mother when we get home and see what she knows about our family's history."

"Aha! You're hooked."

Jane sipped her wine. "Well, maybe a little."

"Let's look at Doris's file."

Jane went and got it and, removing the papers, put them into tidy piles. The first pile was the census reports, which Shelley enjoyed as much as Jane had. "Look at the size of the families!" she exclaimed. "Good Lord! Here's a woman who says she's forty-six years old, and she has a four-year-old child at home as well as a twenty-four-year-old and a dozen in between! Twenty years of steady childbearing."

Jane was studying another sheet. "This one's odd. The mother is twenty-seven, but there's a child of fifteen. That doesn't seem likely."

"It doesn't seem *nice,* either," Shelley said. "No, look. The husband is forty. I'll bet these older ones are his children from a previous marriage. At least I hope so. See, the children are fifteen, thirteen, eleven, and then there's a gap, then a six-year-old and a three-year-old."

"I wonder who she was looking for on these," Jane said. "There isn't any highlighting or notation on the back of any of the reports. Where are they from?"

Shelley shuffled the papers. "One from a township in New York State. One from Denver—no, two from Denver. And one that looks like a farm community in Colorado someplace."

"How can you tell it's a farm community?" Jane asked.

"For one thing, all the men give their occupation as farmer."

Jane laughed. "I think that's a good way of guessing. I'm not sure I'm cut out to be a genealogist. Do you see any names that mean anything to you?"

Shelley ran a finger down the left column of each page. "I don't think so. Some of the names in the farm one look vaguely Russian or Slavic, but no Romanovs or even a Smith."

As Shelley folded up the census reports, Jane handed her the pile of clippings and photos. "Some of these aren't even in English," Shelley complained.

"No, but they each have a number written on the back. There are translations in the stack of paperwork. Most are Romanov cousins and people from Holnagrad, according to Doris's translations."

"Here's an obituary of Gregory Smith."

"Yes, but don't get excited," Jane warned her. "It doesn't tell much of anything about him. Just that he came from Europe and arrived in the community in the 1920s. Most of it's about his late wife, who was connected to the town. I'd guess that either Bill or his sister gave the information to the paper, and they either didn't know much more or were respecting their father's lifelong secrecy and didn't say what they knew."

"I wonder if this Sergei person in the portrait photograph with the Tsar is supposed to be Gregory's father."

"I have no idea."

"What else do you have there?" Shelley carefully bundled up the clippings and pictures and traded them for a thin sheaf of papers Jane had put together with a paper clip.

"Some of it is translations of the clippings. There are a lot that seem to be typed-up transcripts of interviews with old-timers around here who claimed to remember Gregory Smith."

"Have you read them all?"

"Only skimmed them, I'm afraid."

"Okay, you take half. I'll take half."

They dutifully read in silence for a while. Katie strolled through, stared at them for a minute, and said, "You look like you're doing homework. Want to do some of mine when we get home?"

"In your dreams, kiddo," Jane answered.

"Can't hurt to ask," Katie replied breezily.

"What's this about?" Shelley asked, handing Jane the typed sheet with the lists of names and book and page numbers.

"I don't know, except what it says. Sheepshead Bay court records."

"I can see why the two names are starred," Shelley said. "Roman and the one Smith name. Maybe that's the court where Gregor changed his name. If he did. But I wonder why one Smith is starred and the other one isn't. And why did she record the rest of these names?"

Jane understood these to be rhetorical questions and didn't answer. Instead she just put the page on her lap and gazed at it.

A moment later, she gasped.

"What's wrong?"

Jane sat with her mouth open for a minute, then said, "Did you see those greeting cards in the gift shop? The ones with the busy little repetitive patterns on them and you're supposed to stare at them for a long time and imagine you're looking *through* the page—"

"Yes, I think they're a Communist plot to brainwash people like you into thinking you're seeing a secret message."

"But I did see the message on them. And I have a feeling I'm seeing one here. Sort of through the page, if you know what I mean."

"I have no idea what you mean!"

"Look at the list. Look at the names that *aren't* starred. You're right. There's a reason for the rest of the names!"

Shelley went through the list and looked back at Jane blankly. "No secret message."

"Wait a minute. Let me think this out before I open my mouth and make a complete fool of myself," Jane said. She got up and paced for a few moments. Shelley waited patiently, pouring herself another scant tablespoonful of wine and putting another log on the fire.

Finally Jane sat back down and took a deep breath. "I think I know."

She talked for five minutes straight, pointed out the evidence of her theory in Doris's notes and with two other objects; then she sat back, feeling mentally exhausted.

"If this is right—and I suspect it is—I have two questions," Shelley said.

"Fire away."

"Don't sound so cocky," Shelley warned. "First, how did Bill Smith know?"

"Doris told him," Jane said smugly.

"But why would she?"

"Because she was a blabbermouth. She assumed since she found it interesting, everybody would. And Bill did. He found it useful, too. Next question?"

"You can really be insufferable," Shelley said mildly. "Next question is, how do we prove it?"

Jane's smug expression faded. "Gee—I don't know. Hmmm. Oh! Remember when Lucky was talking about professional genealogists in Salt Lake City?

People you can hire to do your research? That's how. We hire a genealogist."

"And get put at the bottom of a list that'll take three months to work up to the top of."

"I believe that's where we have to get Mel into this. He is a professional detective, you know. And he could say so to someone without having to be specific about whether or not he's officially involved in this case."

Shelley cocked an eyebrow doubtfully. "I don't think he's going to like this one little bit."

"Well, if worse comes to worse, we'll have to tell the whole theory to the sheriff and get his people to ask someone there to do it."

"Okay, third question—"

"You said you only had two!"

"I thought of another one. And this is a big one. If the fact we're basing this on is true, it doesn't necessarily prove murder."

"Not just one fact, Shelley. A whole host of them. But I see your point. I think the shock treatment is the only way."

"And how do you plan to administer this shock without getting yourself killed? I like your kids, but I don't want to raise them for you."

Jane thought for a long moment, then raised her hand like a child who suddenly knows the answer to a question. "HawkHunter is doing a reading from his book tomorrow night. Don't you think we could get everybody to attend?"

Shelley frowned. "Maybe so. You really think we can get all our ducks in a row by then? It's less than twenty-four hours away."

Jane lighted a cigarette and started pacing again.

She stopped at the sliding glass doors to the deck and looked up toward Flattop Mountain. "I'll bet—" She broke off, stared at the cigarette in her hand, and then back at the mountain. "Omigod! Shelley! I've got the rest of it, too! Mel was right! It was self-defense *and* money! Oh, Shelley, we have so much to do first thing in the morning. For one thing, we have to find that skier in the red oufit!"

"I'm sure this is going to make some kind of sense when you quit gasping and snorting and explain yourself," Shelley said.

"Oh, it will. It sure will!"

23

In the end, it became necessary to explain to the sheriff. There was simply too much to do in one day that required the authority of law—or at least the seeming authority. The sheriff, to his credit, went along with Jane's plan. It wasn't so much that he believed her as it was pure and simple desperation. Although he didn't admit as much, he and his men were getting nowhere fast and he regarded any possible solution as better than none.

"He's just hedging his bets," Mel said. "If you're right, you might deliver a confessed murderer to him. If you're wrong, you've made a fool of yourself and he's got nothing to do with it except to witness it."

"You think so?" Jane asked as they headed down the road to the main complex of the resort.

"I'm sure of it. You've got everything, haven't you?"

Jane glanced through the canvas bag she carried, ticking off in her mind the items she needed and double-checking that each was in its properly labeled envelope. "I think so. I hope so."

"You're sure you don't want me to do this?"

"No, I'm fine."

That was a lie. Her stomach was in a knot; she was trembling with nerves. She couldn't wait for this to be over. She was certain the information she'd compiled pointed to only one conclusion, but whether she could pile it up effectively enough to elicit a confession was a different matter entirely. A person who could cold-bloodedly murder two other individuals was capable of anything—even brazening out an open threat.

In addition to nerves, she was suffering from weariness. She hadn't been able to sleep at all the night before because her mind had kept racing around and around. And today had started early. A long, frustrating interview with the sheriff and with several other people. Phone calls. A long trudge up to the top of Flattop Mountain. More phone calls.

Fortunately, Shelley had taken charge of the kids—keeping tabs on them, making sure they were entertained and out of the way. She'd even taken them to town and rented two complete sets of videos—everything she could find with Michael J. Fox for the girls and a half-dozen Sylvester Stallone films for the boys. It was she who ordered in vast quantities of pizza as well. Now the kids were all safely locked in their respective condos, gorging themselves and watching movies, and Shelley, Jane, and Mel were on their way to HawkHunter's reading.

It appeared to be surprisingly well attended. That shouldn't have been a surprise, Jane realized. The resort was still swarming with genealogists and they tended to be interested in history of any time and place. And the sheriff had "requested" that a number of people attend who might not otherwise have done so.

They entered the conference room and took seats halfway back along the aisle by the inside wall. At first glance, the room was a "Study in Black and White." More than half the audience were members of the tribe, most of whom Jane had never seen. They were quiet, dignified people, with a few unusually well-behaved children scattered throughout the group. Contrasting with their dark hair were many heads of white hair, belonging to the genealogists, who tended to be of "mature" years. There was a pleasant undertone of conversation as everyone waited for the program to begin. Jane glanced around, "taking roll."

Tenny Garner and Joanna Smith were sitting at the other end of the same row as Jane's group. Tenny was looking haggard and appeared a good ten years older than when Jane had arrived a few days ago. She was sitting with her hands folded in her lap, looking down at them as if deep in thought. The pose gave her an unfortunate suggestion of a double chin.

Joanna, beside her niece, was talking and crocheting as if nothing were wrong. As if nothing had ever been wrong. But as she watched the older woman, Jane realized that her posture was stiff, and Joanna paused several times to put her crochet hook down and flex her fingers. So there was tension there. She was trying to suppress and ignore it, but wasn't succeeding completely.

Pete Andrews had chosen not to sit with his family. Well, they weren't really his family, after all. He was Bill's nephew, not related to Joanna and Tenny except through Bill's marriage. He was talking breezily with a guest, all smiles and rah-rah enthusiasm. He had a black eye and a cut lip from his fight with HawkHunter, but was making light of both, covering his eye with his hand and mugging comically. But as the guest turned away to find a place to sit, Pete's face went blank and became sullen, as if someone had erased the chalk drawing of cheerfulness.

Jane didn't want to appear too nervous about whether everyone was there, so she gazed with apparent calm at the front of the room for a few minutes. HawkHunter was in place already, sitting beside and a little behind the podium with Little Feather next to him. He had a book in his lap with slips of paper protruding. She was dressed this evening in designer jeans and a turquoise silk blouse and wore a fortune in silver-and-turquoise jewelry. She had white feathers and beads woven into her hair. They were talking together in a sporadic, relaxed manner.

Jane heard Lucky behind her as he and Stu Gortner came in. Thank God!

"I don't really know. I'll have to consult with the board and probably have to take the matter to a vote of the membership," Lucky was saying in what was, for him, a very sharp, cranky tone. "I've told you, it's far too important to be decided here and now. We'll have to study the Society's bylaws first to see if they even allow us to become involved in a commercial venture. And even if they do, I doubt the membership will approve of taking what could be construed as a political stand."

"Not even to financially benefit the group?" Stu wheedled.

If Lucky responded, Jane couldn't hear it. When she glanced around, they had taken seats two rows back.

Thomas Whitewing and Linda Moosefoot were directly across the room from Jane. Their heads were together, their glossy blue-black hair appearing to mingle as they whispered to each other. Linda looked up, caught Jane's eye, and grinned. Jane tried to smile back, but her face was frozen with nerves. She glanced away quickly.

The woman who ran the bookstore came in, looking vaguely perplexed.

There were three people missing. Three important people.

"Where's the sheriff?" Jane whispered to Mel.

"In the hall outside. I keep catching a glimpse of him. He's out of uniform, that's why you didn't notice him."

That accounted for one of them.

Shelley nudged Jane. "Here she is!"

Jane breathed a sign of relief as the second, a tall, tanned woman, came into the room. She was thin, with severely short blond hair and a strong, graceful, mannish stride. She crossed the room at the front and sat down in the second row without any dithering or hesitation. She folded her arms across her chest and sat staring ahead at the front wall. No one spoke to her or seemed to recognize her.

Including Mel. "Who's that?" he asked in a low voice.

"Susan Maxwell. You know, the mysterious skier I kept seeing on the mountain," Jane replied. "I told you Shelley and I 'ambushed' her early this morning up there."

Practically on her heels, a huge middle-aged Indian in a red plaid shirt came in and took a seat in the first row. Linda Moosefoot looked at Jane, pointed to the man, and nodded. He was the third necessary person.

Thomas Whitewing rose and approached the podium, tapping the microphone. Apparently it wasn't working and he looked at HawkHunter. HawkHunter made an eloquent motion indicating that it was all right, that he didn't need it anyway.

Thomas turned to the audience. "Tonight we are fortunate," he shouted, then, catching Linda's signal, glanced at his notes and lowered his voice. "We are fortunate to have a noted author, HawkHunter, with us to read from his masterwork, *I, HawkHunter*. This book was a *New York Times* best-seller for over a year, three months of that time in the number-one slot. This work, a slightly fictionalized account of HawkHunter's own heritage, spoke to our country and to the world about the life and history of America's first people.

"HawkHunter will read some selected passages and will then entertain questions and discussion from the audience. I'm honored to present John Hawk-Hunter."

Thomas, looking proud but relieved, went back to sit down by Linda, and HawkHunter took the podium.

He read from four different sections of the book. A superb speaker, he gathered the audience in immediately with his rich, beautiful voice. The sections he chose were both profoundly poetic and troublingly inflammatory. Perhaps the whole book was, Jane thought, sorry she hadn't had time to reread it all before attending this presentation. The first part he read was from the viewpoint of a medicine woman in the sixteen-hundreds, meeting the first white men the tribe had ever seen. In a few paragraphs, the listener got to know her, to recognize her wisdom and the respect the tribe had for her, and just as quickly was made to cringe at the ignorant, lumpish whites and their dismissive, if not downright lewd, regard of her.

The second and third sections HawkHunter read were much the same, albeit of different individuals and different time periods, but with the same theme: the superior Indian—spiritual, intelligent, and inherently noble and courteous—and the marauding whites—crass, greedy, and stupid.

For a moment Jane got so caught up in the content of the reading that she almost forgot that her purpose here was not to have a literary or cultural experience, but to unmask a killer. HawkHunter's reading was, to Jane at least, only a reason for her to assemble the people needed for her plan. Still, she found herself wondering what effect this provocative material was having.

She knew the stone-faced Indian was a stereotype, but at that moment it was quite true of the people in this room. None of the tribe members whose faces she could see were overtly registering any emotion at all—no hint of a smile, no suggestion of a frown. The others, the genealogists and other resort guests, all looked slightly distressed. Their expressions ranged from sympathy to guilt to anger.

HawkHunter opened the book to another page and read a passage about himself as a child. A very different piece—at first. It was about the joy of being a boy who was part of the land, nature, and a nurturing extended family. It was a charming, romping, happy story, and then it veered off into an account of some drunken white cowboys wandering onto the tribal land and raping his young aunt. It ended with HawkHunter, as an eight-year-old boy, hiding behind a rock so that the elders wouldn't see him cry.

He finished reading, closed the book, and shut his eyes for a moment as if overcome by the emotion of the experience all over again. Then, as a fitful spatter of applause started and quickly grew, he opened his eyes, made a suggestion of a bow, and said, "Are there questions now? Or anything in particular someone would like to discuss?"

Jane stood quickly. "Mr. HawkHunter, I notice you're still missing your tooth. I found it in the snow. Would you like to have it to give to your dentist?"

There was a ruffle of sound. A little bit of amusement, some tutting disapproval.

"I appreciate that, but you're mistaken. My tooth was broken, but not lost. Other questions—?"

"No, I believe this is your tooth," Jane said, holding up a tissue that was folded and taped.

Little Feather had risen, scowling, and come hastily down the side aisle. When she reached Jane, she snatched at the little package roughly and went back to the podium. HawkHunter was looking at Jane with contemptuous amusement. "Well, ma'am, if you say so," he said with a laugh. He pointed to someone in the audience who was holding her hand up to be called on.

Jane felt her face flush, but Shelley nudged her and she went on, overriding the woman who was attempting to ask about HawkHunter's research. "Mr. HawkHunter, the odd thing about that tooth is that it doesn't belong to an Indian."

He glanced at her with irritation. "Certainly not this Indian," he said. He turned to the other questioner. "My research began with a childhood of stories, stories told by my grandmother and grandfather—"

"What were their names—your grandparents'?" Jane all but shouted.

"Look here, lady, I don't know what you're trying to do, but you're disrupting this meeting and I suggest you find someplace else to go."

"How about the Sheepshead Bay court?" Jane asked. "They have very interesting records, you know."

At that, HawkHunter grabbed the podium with one hand as if to keep his balance. "I don't know what—"

"I think you do," Jane said. "Let me tell you about one of those records." She had the sheet of fax paper in her hand and ready. She held it up and said, "This is a copy of the record of Johan Aulkunder changing his name to John HawkHunter on his eighteenth birthday. And this"—she flourished another sheet of paper—"is a picture of Johan Aulkunder in his high school yearbook. Even on a fax, it's apparent how much he resembles the picture of you on the back of your book. Of course, neither of those pictures resembles you today very much. You've had a lot of plastic surgery, haven't you, Mr. HawkHunter? But you couldn't change the shape of your teeth, or the characteristics of your skull. It's very easy to disprove American Indian heritage. And Doris Schmidtheiser knew that. She was very indiscreet, too, and mentioned to you that she'd found this record when she was rummaging around for evidence of Gregor Roman changing his name."

HawkHunter's mouth was working, but words wouldn't come. He turned and looked at Little Feather. She ripped open the little tissue package and held up a small, hard item. "This is just a rock!" she said, flinging it toward Jane. Her aim was bad. Frantic. The bit of gravel pinged off the wall.

The room was deathly still. HawkHunter groped to recover the situation. "This is exactly the kind of libelous nonsense the whites have always used on Indians! The nitpicking pseudo-science that is meant to discredit. Next she'll be spouting nonsense about brain size—"

The dauntingly large man in the red plaid shirt in the front row had stood up and joined him at the podium. He took hold of HawkHunter's arm in a vise-like grip. "I'd like to hear what more this lady has to say," he said in a deep voice.

"What I'm saying is this: that man is no more a Native American than I am," Jane replied. "In fact, I've probably got a couple of generations on him as far as our tenure in America goes."

There was a nasty undertone in the room. Whether it was directed at her or HawkHunter or both of them, Jane couldn't guess.

"Don't you see, Leon, what's she's trying to do?" HawkHunter said. "Just what the whites have always done—tried to turn us against our own people. And once again it's working! You can't believe her! You're betraying your own people!"

"It's easy to prove," Jane said. "Will you agree to have a skull X-ray and your teeth examined?"

"No! He will not!" Little Feather shrilled. "He doesn't have to prove a damned thing to you, you white bitch!"

This time the rumble of discontent had a clear target. Little Feather had made a big mistake.

"Maybe not, but he has to prove it to me," the big man named Leon said. He still had a grip on HawkHunter's arm and was looking down at him.

"Excuse me, sir, but are you Leon Whitewing? The president of the tribal council?" Jane asked.

"I am."

"Then it was you who signed the contract with HawkHunter on behalf of the tribe," Jane said, brandishing a copy that Linda Moosefoot had made for her.

"I did," Leon Whitewing said.

"Would you give the gist of that contract?"

"I don't see why not. It's not a secret. We engaged HawkHunter to represent our interest in regard to the legal ownership of Flattop."

"And what are you paying him for that?" Jane went on.

"Nothing," Leon said. "It's a pro bono situation."

"Is it?" Jane asked.

Leon responded slowly, as if his mind were running about ten times as fast as his mouth. "Well, officially he's to get ten percent of the profits from anything that's done with the land if he wins the suit. But since we'll just restore it to its cemetery status—"

He seemed startled as the tall woman in the second row whipped her head around to look at Jane. Jane nodded to her and the woman stood up.

"Mr. Whitewing, this is Susan Maxwell," Jane said. "You may have seen her around lately in a red ski outfit. She's with a firm of architectural engineers. Susan, would you tell Mr. Whitewing what you've been doing?"

Susan Maxwell glared for a long minute at HawkHunter, then said, "Since it appears that I'm going to get stiffed for my fees in all likelihood, I might as well. John HawkHunter hired me to look over the

summit of the hill you call Flattop Mountain and
draw up preliminary plans for a casino complex to be
built there."

There wasn't a stony face in the room anymore.
Everyone was either stunned or confused and frankly
showed it.

Jane explained. "Tribal lands—reservations—are
federal lands. They aren't subject to state laws. It's
possible that if HawkHunter had gotten that land declared part of the tribal land—either through legal
methods or by intimidation—a very large gambling
operation could have gone up on the hill. A large and
extremely profitable operation, of which he would
have received a percentage for the rest of his life."

Little Feather was edging toward the door. The sheriff shifted himself directly in front of the doorway and
folded his arms. HawkHunter had been trying to gently
extricate himself from Leon Whitewing's grasp, but
now he gave a great lurch sideways. Leon didn't
loosen his grip and jerked HawkHunter back like a rag
doll.

"You've got a lot to explain to the tribe—white
boy!" Leon said.

"He's got a lot to explain to the sheriff, too," Jane
said. "About the deaths of Doris Schmidtheiser and
Bill Smith."

—— 24 ——

There was a big table set in the dining room and Jane had been urged to sit at the head of it. Tenny had arranged for desserts, coffee, and brandy to be served, and was now sitting with the group, which included Linda Moosefoot and Thomas Whitewing as well as his uncle Leon. Lucky had managed to lose Stu Gortner in order to join them, and the bookstore owner had come along too.

". . . a lot of things," Jane was saying. "And they all came together at once. Linda had called Little Feather a professional Indian, and Shelley and I had laughed at HawkHunter's vanity in making himself look more typically Indian. But I hadn't put those two things together until I was staring at that list of names Doris had in her notes. I'd looked at them several times and they didn't mean anything. Then I started mumbling them out loud. And suddenly I realized that while 'Aulkunder' and 'HawkHunter' don't look anything alike, they sound alike."

"Lucky helped us contact a genealogist in Brooklyn to run down and look at the original records this morning," Shelley said. "And sure enough, they showed that it was him. As it turns out, this man is a teacher at the high school Johan Aulkunder attended. He called around to some of the older teachers and put together an interesting profile of the boy who turned himself into HawkHunter."

"Profile? What do you mean?" Tenny asked.

"According to the teachers who remember him," Shelley explained, "he was one of those sad, shy, brilliant loners who created a fantasy life for himself. He'd lived in a series of foster homes and, maybe because he had no real family of his own, became obsessed with Indians. Read every book in the library about them. Drew headdresses in his notebooks, had a vast collection of arrowheads, that sort of thing."

Jane picked up the story. "The day he turned eighteen, he changed his name and moved away. Nobody at the school had any idea what had become of him, and by the time he made a name for himself, it was a different name, with a more mature and possibly already slightly altered appearance. No one made the connection."

Leon Whitewing was nodding. "I understand now about the book."

"What do you mean, Uncle Leon?" Thomas asked. He was still looking very upset at the crumbling of HawkHunter's image.

Leon had a battered copy of the book with him. He opened it to the introduction and jabbed his finger at the last paragraph. "He says here that while the book is true in essence, he's altered the name of the tribe and the personal names of his relatives to protect both the tribe and his own family from unwanted public attention. But that wasn't why. It was because it was all a lie!"

The lady from the bookstore was sitting next to him and spoke up. "Now, Leon, that's not really fair. He probably meant it as fiction to begin with and put

that in as a sort of flourish. Like Waller did—
claiming he learned the story of Francesca and
what's-his-name from the family."

Leon looked at her blankly. "Waller? Francesca?"

"Never mind, Leon. I just mean lots of authors add
things like that to give the fiction a greater semblance
of realism. And from what Mrs. Jeffry says about his
background, the book probably started out as a way
of recording a fantasy that was terribly important to
him. Imagine this lonely boy with no real family in-
venting a family for himself. Generations of family.
But the fantasy became a book and the book took off
and he was suddenly a figure of respect, almost idol-
atry. He got trapped in his own lie."

"Which he probably didn't mind," Leon said
grumpily.

"Who would mind?" Jane said. "We'd all like that
kind of adoration. Not to mention the income that
went with it."

"I still don't understand how Mrs. Schmidtheiser
came into it all," Tenny said.

"She was a snoop," Jane said. "That's all. She was
rummaging around in some records and saw his name
change. She made a note of it, and quite innocently
mentioned it to him. In fact, I think I probably saw
her do it right here in this room. She was with him
at a table where he was sitting alone. I assumed she
was haranguing him to come to the debate later that
day. He looked taken aback and I thought it was just
from the force of her personality, but it was probably
shock that she'd found out his deepest, most dangerous secret. He had to silence her."

Lucky shook his head. "Poor Doris. She was obsessed with celebrities and never caught on that most

of them didn't like her delving into their pasts. I'll bet most of the rest of the people on that list changed their names to something we'd recognize."

"I think she was showing him that list when I thought she was trying to get him interested in the debate. That's how he knew what to look for in her cabin. But he had no way of knowing she'd dropped it and I'd picked it up."

"Like Mel said to us last night, being an Indian had become his lifework," Shelley said. "His income, the prestige he'd become dependent on even more than the money—his whole way of life was precariously balanced on a lie. And here was this strange, babbling woman who knew the lie and was shooting off her mouth about it and flinging around documents that proved it in a public dining room where anyone might hear."

"But wasn't she poisoned with her own heart pills?" the bookstore woman asked. "How did he do that?"

"I don't know for sure," Jane answered, "but I can imagine one scenario. Everybody had seen her popping those pills like they were breath mints. If he went to her condo to talk over what she'd found out, she'd have been fawning all over him. If she went to the kitchen to fix him coffee, he could have gotten the pills from her bag. And then, when the coffee was on the table, all he'd have had to do was ask for something else—cream or sugar, maybe—and she'd have run right back into the kitchen. It wouldn't have taken a second to drop them in her cup while she was gone."

"And then just sit there and wait?" Linda Moosefoot asked with a shudder.

Tenny said, "But how on earth did Uncle Bill get involved?"

Jane looked at Mel, who had been allowed to go to the police station immediately following the reading and subsequent revelations.

"She told Bill," he said. "That's all. And Bill mentioned knowing it."

"When?" Tenny asked.

"When he went for a walk and HawkHunter caught up with him in the woods at the edge of the bunny slope. HawkHunter was probably making some new threat in regard to his lawsuit, and Bill used this shiny new weapon—the truth about HawkHunter's real background. HawkHunter killed him then and there," Mel said. "It seems that HawkHunter was actually a guest here, which Jane and I didn't know. And his condo was the closest to the spot where Mr. Smith was killed."

"I knew, of course," Tenny said, "but never had any reason to mention it. You never asked. How do you know what happened between them?"

"From Little Feather," Mel said. "She's talking as loud and fast as she can to try to save herself from going down with HawkHunter's ship. She says the weapon was one of those indestructible plastic thermos bottles. He threw it into the woods. They may not find it until the spring melt."

Linda Moosefoot spoke again. "But why the snowman?"

Mel shrugged. "The easiest way to hide the body, I suppose. HawkHunter had to put it someplace, and concealing it right on the spot was a whole lot easier than carrying it around. Simply heaping snow on top would have looked suspicious, and as soon as Bill was known to be missing, somebody would have gotten curious. But the snowman could have stood there for weeks if Jane hadn't run into it."

Linda still wasn't satisfied. "But why the robe and crown? To implicate somebody from the genealogy group?"

Jane shook her head. "I think that was just a fortunate coincidence for him. I think the blanket was just because it was so hard to get the snow to stick together. With the blanket, he only had to cover half the body. As for the fruit bowl, I don't know. Maybe just an afterthought. Possibly even Little Feather's idea when she saw what he'd done and realized the blanket looked like a royal cape."

They fell silent for a moment. A waiter approached the table with a box, which he handed to Tenny. "Thanks, Kevin," she said, rising and taking the box around the table to Jane.

"What's this?" Jane asked.

"Oh, just something I thought you'd like," Tenny said, preoccupied.

Jane opened the box and discovered it contained the set of small bowls Tenny had said were being fired to match the bowl Jane had purchased. Surprised and pleased, she thanked Tenny effusively, and as soon as she'd stopped gushing, the party started breaking up.

Leon Whitewing stood majestically. "Well, he sure fooled a bunch of dumb Indians, I'll say that for the bastard."

"Leon, he fooled everybody," Tenny said. "You know, if he'd just told the truth—that he wanted the top of the reservation land so the tribe could build a casino—it wouldn't have necessarily been a bad thing. The tribe could have made a fortune, and the resort would have been the logical place for a bunch of rich gamblers to stay."

Leon grinned. "You got a point there, Tenny."

"I do, don't I?" she said, her face lighting up. "It would be another good reason for people to stay at a ski resort that has almost no ski facilities."

Leon took her arm in a courtly manner. "We've got some things to talk about."

They all said their good-nights and Jane, Mel, and Shelley trudged up the hill to their cabins. When they got to the one Jane and Shelley were sharing with the girls, there was a commotion going on in the living room.

"What's wrong!" Jane asked, alarmed. The girls were squatting on the living room floor next to each other.

Katie moved aside and revealed Willard with a collection of bandages stuck on his muzzle. "Mom, I let Willard out and he caught up with that white cat. It beat him up, then rolled him around in the snow." She was trying to stifle her giggles and sound sympathetic.

"Poor old Willard," Jane said.

He whined in response.

"Well, he'll have tomorrow to recover. We'd all better get to bed so we can get up early," Jane said.

As they filed down the hallway, Shelley said, "Did you see the way Tenny acted about the casino idea?"

Jane started shedding clothing. "I sure did. I think she's getting more interested in the idea of running the resort. What about Paul and the other investors? Are they still interested in buying it?"

"I'm afraid with the casino idea, it probably just

went out of their price range. Which is okay with me. As nice as this place is, I don't think I'd ever want to come back."

When they'd both undressed, gotten into their beds, and turned out the lights, Shelley said sleepily, "Jane, there's still one thing I wonder about. And I don't think we'll ever know."

"What's that, Shelley?" Jane asked, yawning.

"What the hell the sheriff's name really is."